DEMONCON

D.W. DIBLING

DIBLING
SCRIBBLING
LTD. CO.

First Printing, 2017

ISBN 978-0-9916215-6-9 (paperback)

ISBN 978-0-9916215-7-6 (eBook)

Dibling Scribbling Ltd. Co.

438 Crystal Lake Road

Rebecca, GA 31783

www.DiblingScribbling.com

For Dena,

Who believes in me even when I don't.

Dear Reader,

While, of course, this book is a work of fiction and the events portrayed are strictly the creation of the author's overwrought imagination —did I mention he has broken bones over imagined ghosts?— the inspiration for these imaginings came from a real-life event.

If you're not aware, the city of Atlanta, Georgia, hosts an annual "multi-genre" convention known as Dragon Con, which has grown from humble roots of 1,400 attendees in 1987 to over 77,000 in 2016, one of whom was yours truly.

The convention is amazing! The level of dedication and effort that some of the attendees show is breath-taking, and if you ever go to the conference, you will see characters in costumes so elaborate that they might have walked straight off a movie set. Some as simple as a T-shirt with a slogan painted on it. The size of the crowds I have tried to depict is no exaggeration. The convention halls and the sidewalks outside simply teem with surging masses of costumed revelers, mixed with an almost equal amount of Atlanteans confused over the sudden change in the downtown streets.

I have gleefully attended Dragon Con for several years now. Mostly I go just to watch, though I do enjoy dressing up as one of my favorite television characters. But it was the level of professionalism in some of the costumes that gave me the spark of inspiration for this book. While shuffling down one of the many packed hallways of a hotel hosting the 'con, I walked around a corner and nearly bumped into one of the more inspired costumes, something straight out of a nightmare. And, suddenly, I was struck with the thought, "What if one of these monsters was real? How would you know?"

From that initial glimmer, after far too much time in gestation, this book has finally emerged. I hope you enjoy it. I enjoyed thinking about it and struggling with its birth. After all, what is life without a little bit of mystery, a little bit of the unexplained?

Prologue

I N THE EARLY MORNING hours, the building began to shake, almost violently. Atlanta is no stranger to tremors, but normally, they are almost imperceptible. The kind of quake where you question whether or not you really felt anything at all. Usually, you decide that you're just imagining things and go along your merry way. But not this time. This time there was a definite, sharp shudder and a distant rumble. In the posh downtown hotel, the lights went out, and the emergency lighting flickered on. Warning indicators began blinking in the maintenance office, located in an out of the way corner of the ground floor, as if the general lack of lighting wasn't enough of a clue that there was an electrical problem.

"Did you feel that?" asked Bob, just about to go home after a long, uneventful night shift.

"Hell, yes, I felt that," said his relief, Pete, the maintenance supervisor. "Get down to the basement and check out the breakers."

"But my shift's almost over," Bob complained. Although he wanted to go home, it was more that he didn't want to go down to the basement by himself. It's not so much that he had seen things in the basement, though there were rats. Bob didn't like rats. But he always had a feeling in the basement. A feeling he couldn't describe, couldn't really put a finger on, but the feelings were there just the same. The kind of feelings that made the hair stand up on his neck and left him clammy and itchy, feelings that made him queasy. And then there were the sounds. Strange rumblings and groanings, as though the hotel's belly was slightly upset with its latest meal. Bob often thought that the basement was examining *him* as its next meal, and that never made him feel good. *Or*, he thought, *maybe I make the basement a little queasy.*

"Looks like you're going to get some overtime now. C'mon, I'll go with you." Pete eyed Bob with a jaded eye. He knew why Bob didn't want to go to the basement. *This younger generation really is a bunch of pansies*, he thought. *No stomach*, he thought. *No back-bone. It's a wonder they get anything done at all.*

The two men dug flashlights out of a desk drawer and left the office. Knowing the elevators wouldn't work on emergency power, they walked passed the service elevator just outside the office, opened a stairwell door marked "Authorized Personnel Only," and headed down the service stairs. Bob didn't like the stairwells when the lights were on. They were dirty and dank and sometimes he found rats that glared at him like *he* was the trespasser. In the narrow beam of the flashlights, the stairs became downright sinister. Shadows danced a jerky dance. Shapes took on stretched, angular forms and Bob's stomach tightened and twisted in disturbing ways. *At least I'm not alone*, he thought.

They had to go down three flights from the ground floor to reach the sub-basement where the electrical power entered the building through a large breaker box. The air seemed to grow colder with each passing step, footsteps crunching in the gritty dust that was almost as thick as a carpet runner. Their jerking progress made the flashlight beams swing wildly, causing an even more skittish dance of the shadows on the walls. Bob felt as though he might be sick. Finally, they reached the basement level and pushed open the access door.

The emergency lighting was on in the basement, too, though some of the fixtures needed to have bulbs replaced and so provided no illumination at all. *I'm going to hear about that*, thought Bob. The light was dim and uneven, and the air was filled with a fine dust that turned the light from their flashlights into long, white cones that faded into the inky distance. They could hear a muffled sound far ahead in the blackness, a gentle sighing with sinister undertones. Bob was getting that feeling again. The basement definitely seemed hungry this morning.

Bob coughed nervously and said, "That was some earthquake. I don't think I've ever felt one like that before."

"No," said Pete. "Me, neither. Must've shifted some of the electrical and knocked out the power. And the convention starts today. I don't know how we'll get things up and running in time." Bob groaned inwardly. He knew how. He would spend long hours in the basement working on the electrical system. As far as Bob was concerned, overtime was great. Overtime in the basement was something else altogether.

They walked down the hall toward the main electrical distribution block. They could hear crackling, and the air felt charged with static electricity. Electric bolts snapped and arced stroboscopically, forcing them to squint. A cold draft blasted down the hall from the direction of the block, and as they approached, they could see that part of the wall had been blown out, rubble scattered across the hall. The wind grew stronger as they approached the breach and they had to walk more carefully now, leaning into the wind and picking their way through the debris.

"Where is this air coming from?" Bob yelled above the howl of the wind.

"I don't know," yelled the supervisor in reply. "There's no subway or tunneling that I know of that runs anywhere near here."

They looked into the gaping crater. It looked as though a truck had driven through the wall, but instead of being filled with dirt or bedrock, as they expected to see, the hole seemed to open onto a Stygian abyss. Blue lightning flashed around the edges of the void and the icy blast issued from the center. Next to the hole in the wall was the main electrical distribution block, untouched except that the main circuit breakers were tripped to the "off" position. They looked at each other, confusion apparent on their faces.

They aimed their flashlights into the cavity, but the light seemed to be absorbed and revealed nothing. Bob reset the main breakers by pushing them to "on." The circuit breaker gave a loud clunk, and the emergency lights winked out as the regular lights flickered on. Suddenly the wind died, and the lightning dwindled and crackled out. As the howling of the wind subsided, another sound became evident. A deep rumbling, low in pitch and volume; a warning growl that could only be produced by a tremendous throat. As the dust began to settle, the two men looked nervously at each other. When they looked back into the void, two dots of yellow light gleamed back at them.

The dots blinked.

There was the roar of an angry beast.

There were the screams of two terrified men.

There was the rattle of two flashlights falling on the floor.

Chapter One

"MARY, WHERE ARE WE?" asked Jane. She paused, leaning on her pitchfork, and took a drink of the blue concoction she was carrying in a long, plastic tumbler hanging by a strap around her neck. "Are we lost?" Tucking a strand of blonde hair behind her ear and adjusting her tail, she looked up and down the hallway.

"Next year, I want a less complicated costume," she said. "This tail is a real pain in my ass." She paused, a comical look on her face. "Get it?" she laughed. "A pain in my ass!"

"Yeah, you're a real laugh riot," said Mary, smiling as she shook her head at her friend's joke. She looked up and down the hall and shook her head again.

"I'm not sure where we are. I think it's that

way," Mary replied, gesturing with her head as she leaned against the wall, adjusting the strap on her left high heel. The hot pink heels matched the pink miniskirt of her anime costume. Mary's outfit was a garish, mostly pink, schoolgirl uniform, complete with a short tie, a poofed-out miniskirt, and frilly, turned down ankle socks over fishnet stockings. Jane was dressed as a devil in a tight, bright red body suit with a tail swinging behind her and a pitchfork being put to use as a walking stick. Mary straightened up, blew a strand of hair out of her face, and adjusted the lacy black masquerade mask that accentuated her eyes.

"Didn't that guy say the bar was around the second left?"

"Second left? I thought he said second right," said Jane. She stood frozen for a moment, holding her tail, and trying to remember the man's directions. "I told you we should've gotten a map. It's too easy to get lost in all these buildings and hallways."

They walked on, stumbling a little, and supporting each other. The hall they were in was mostly deserted, despite the throng that filled most of the hotel. Six hotels were hosting the annual convention, spread across several blocks of downtown Atlanta, and there were thousands, even tens of thousands, of people in attendance. Most were in costume, and even before ten in the morning, many were in some state of inebriation. DemonCon was in full swing, and people had come from all over the United States to dress in costumes of their favorite sci-fi or fantasy movie, comic book, or television show. Some people had even come from as far away as Europe and Japan. Costumes ranged from a simple T-shirt and mask to elaborate mechanical monstrosities that had lights, sound effects, and sometimes even smoke generators. Some people came just to see all the costumes rather than attend the sessions of the convention or go to see the movie and television stars in the "Hall of Fame." In most places, the convention hotels were so packed that pushing through crowds was the rule, rather than the exception, and "excuse me," was the most common phrase of the weekend. Having spent most of the last day pushing through a seemingly never-ending throng of people, Mary knew the fact that the hallway they were in was empty was not a good sign. They were clearly far away from the main convention areas.

"Damn shoes. I knew I shouldn't have bought these cheap things. Why didn't you stop me?" Mary paused again to adjust the strap of her right heel.

She scowled at Jane even though, in truth, they were best friends. They started coming to DemonCon when they were both freshmen at Georgia Tech and this year marked the fourth year they had attended the 'Con together.

Jane laughed and kept walking. "Because whenever I try to do something like that, you tell me to mind my own business." Jane looked back over her shoulder and said, "Come on Slow Poke! I don't want to miss Happy Hour!"

"How many Happy Hours are there in one day?" asked Mary.

"At least one more, I hope," said Jane with a grin. Mary smiled, too, and they gave each other a high five.

As Jane rounded the corner, she walked right into the demon. It was like walking into the wall. Tall and hulking, his black skin glistening with sweat, the demon snorted at her and glared. A single, jagged horn projected from his forehead. Jane looked up at the jagged spike, her eyes following the red rivulet that looked like blood trickling from the horn, oozing down over the beast's mouth, and dripping from his chin. He wore a shirt with the sleeves raggedly torn off and a pair of pants that were stained and ripped. The hobnails in his boots ground on the tile of the hallway as he shifted slightly, seeking a better footing. His arms seemed to reach below his knees, his entire body of proportions that were not quite up to da Vinci's standards. The mass of his head, shoulders, and chest completely overpowered the rest of his body. The demon drew himself to his full height, towering over the girls, and seemed to fill the hallway.

"Oh, excuse me," said Jane. "Wow! That's an awesome costume!" She looked over the demon admiringly and asked, "Did you make it yourself?"

The demon tucked something into his shirt and narrowed his yellow, pupilless eyes. A low growl rumbled from deep in his chest, and he tilted his head as if considering her question.

"Make…it…yourself," he echoed haltingly. As he spoke, the red liquid dripped onto his shirt, the drops spreading like a crimson spiderweb in the cloth.

"Mary, would you look at this? What a wild costume! That almost looks like real blood!" Jane stood on her toes and reached out to touch the demon's horn, but he jerked his head back a little and pushed her hand away.

"Hey, don't be an asshole," Mary said. "She was

just admiring your costume. We make our own costumes, too. We work on them all year before the 'con." She turned a neat pirouette to show off her handiwork. The demon did not seem to be impressed or, at least if he was, he made no comment. "How long did it take you to put yours together?"

"Put…yours…together," he echoed. Though his eyes had no pupils, the girls could sense his force of concentration. His head swung back and forth looking first at one of the girls and then at the other while he licked the red liquid from his lips. His tongue was long and lizard-like.

"Hey, that's really cool! Like that guy from Kiss. What was his name, Mary? The one that spits fire and blood and stuff." Jane started to play air guitar while sticking her tongue out and nodding her head violently.

"Um, George something, wasn't it?" said Mary. She tilted her head to one side and concentrated. "Sampson. George Sampson, right?"

"Yeah! That's it!" said Jane. "George Sampson." She raised her tumbler to her lips and took another drink. "I…wanna rock and roll…all ni-i-ight! And party ev-er-y-day!" She sang tunelessly, but with great enthusiasm.

Still, the demon remained unenthused. He crossed his gargantuan arms, the muscles of his chest causing his shirt to bulge out. As he flexed, his skin made the sound of leather being stretched to the breaking point. With no pupils, it was hard to tell exactly what he was looking at, but his gaze seemed to harden. A growl rumbled deep in his chest as his breath sighed out of his quivering nostrils.

"I love the contacts," said Jane. "Is this some sort of rubber muscle suit?" she asked and reached her hand out to touch one of his arms.

The demon snorted again and pushed past them, parting the girls like a bowling ball parts pins, knocking Mary down and forcing Jane against the wall. Jane's plastic tumbler shattered from the force of the impact, splashing blue liquid on her and the wall, a puddle forming on the floor.

"Hey! Look out!" said Jane. "My drink!" She shook her arms, slinging more blue liquid on the floor, and then pawed at her hair, trying to shake loose the droplets clinging there.

"Asshole!" Mary yelled after him. Giving him the finger with one hand while she tugged at her miniskirt with the other, she checked herself for any injury.

The demon paid them no further attention and quickly disappeared around the next corner of the hallway. His movements were much more graceful than his vast bulk would suggest, his hobnails making a quiet screeching noise as they ground into the tile. The deep rumble of his breathing faded and in his wake, a sickly sweet, coppery smell hung on the air.

"What a jerk," said Jane. "Here. Let me help you up." She reached down and pulled Mary back to her feet. "Are you ok?" she asked.

"Yeah, I'll be ok. What an ass!" she said, rubbing her hip and straightening her mask again. "Look at this," she said, turning a leg to one side. "He ripped my stockings! Some people just get too much into character, if you ask me."

"Yeah, you got that right," Jane said. She looked wistfully at the remnants of her tumbler and then threw what pieces were left in her hand to the ground. "C'mon, let's find a bathroom so I clean up. This shit is sticky. Then we can find that bar and get another drink."

They walked around the corner and found they had come to a dead end. Two service elevators were the only exits from the hallway. Another costumed attendee was propped up against the far wall, his head back, apparently asleep. Finding people napping throughout the 'con was commonplace. The conference sessions and party schedule favored late nights with little or no sleep at all. People took naps when and where they could.

"Someone's had too much to drink," said Mary, wrinkling her nose at the smells emanating from the sleeper. "Oh, man, he must've dropped his phone, too," she said, pointing to the broken cell phone lying on the floor next to him. "What kind of costume is that supposed to be, anyway?"

"I don't know," said Jane, walking closer to the sleeping man, looking more closely. On his head, he had a helmet of sorts that looked like it was made from a colander. It was wrapped in tin foil, and pipe cleaners came out at random angles. A white wig poked out from under the helmet. Goggles covered his eyes, and his white lab coat had a pocket protector with an assortment of pens, mechanical pencils, and rulers jutting out. There were rubber gloves on his hands and over his shoes were paper booties like a surgeon would wear. Spittle ran down his chin from his open mouth.

"Some kind of mad scientist, I guess. Jeez, how 1950s."

"Yeah, pretty lame." said Mary, "God, he

stinks!" She fanned a hand in the air in front of her nose. "What is this on his chest? Some kind of hole? What kind of mad scientist has a big hole in his chest?"

"I dunno," said Jane. "I don't think I've seen that in any movie."

"It really looks real, though, doesn't it?" Mary said, squatting down to get a closer look. As her eye reached the level of the hole, the white of the wall behind him gleamed out at her.

Her scream echoed down the hallway.

Chapter Two

CONNOR BREEGAN PULLED HIS unmarked cruiser up to the curb under the portico of the hotel, shut off the engine, and stepped out into the crowd. Breegan waved his badge at the concierge who had started forward in protest. As usual, the badge caused the doorman to slink away, muttering under his breath about the abuses of power.

Convention goers were everywhere. The city streets were littered with the costumed freaks and throngs of local who were watching the circus. Breegan was no fan of the convention—a lot of nonsense if you asked him. Grown adults running around in comic book costumes or pretending to be Jedi knights. As a homicide detective in Atlanta, he didn't have much time for comic books or movies.

His idea of relaxing in his rare off-duty time was trying to reach the bottom of a bottle of bourbon. At the bottom, his nightmares were the quietest. The things he had seen on the mean streets could turn a person's hair white overnight.

He paused beside his car to light a cigarette and take in the scene. According to State law, he had to smoke outside the building, and judging by the preliminary reports he had received, he needed to steady his nerves in advance. Breegan was already on edge from his argument with the Police Chief. This was to be handled as quietly as possible. No need to frighten all the tourists who were even now opening their wallets all over downtown Atlanta. While the six hotels of the convention were gathering the lion's share of the debauchery, almost every hotel in the downtown area was booked solid, restaurants were overflowing with customers, and parking garages were full. Breegan didn't agree, but an order was an order. Besides, it was just one murder.

Breegan took one final drag and exhaled through his nose. He squinted through the smoke as he ground the stub into the sidewalk. *Stupid habit*, he thought.

"Why is it the stupid habits are the hardest ones

to break?" he asked of no one in particular. He headed across the pavement and into the hotel.

A uniformed officer was waiting for him at the entrance. "Right this way, sir." The two entered the hotel lobby, a seething mass of loud, colorful, and gridlocked humanity. Walking was difficult and slow, the route circuitous and opportunistic in the crowded space. With the lobby densely packed with people, the sound of a thousand conversations melded into an almost calming hum, like the murmur of the waves at the beach.

The multitude of aromas likewise merged into a unique combination, perfumes and colognes mingled with the scent of food and body odor, that reminded Breegan of the way his grandparent's church social hall would smell during the potluck meal after the Sunday morning service. His parents weren't very religious, but his grandparents never missed a service. The aroma, however, was the only similarity with the church congregation of his childhood memory and the costumed crowd of the convention Breegan realized, as a half-naked nymph, clothed mostly in body paint, squeezed past him. Breegan's mouth watered involuntarily at the odors coming from the hotel's restaurant and the various vendors set up specially for the convention.

It was a bustling bazaar constructed in the middle of a posh hotel lobby.

As Breegan followed the officer through a maze of hallways, the din of the convention faded behind them. Eventually, they came to a corner that was roped off with police tape. A couple more badges were there to keep out the curious, though there didn't seem to be many people in that corner of the hotel. Breegan flashed his badge and ducked under the tape as his escort headed back to the entrance of the hotel. He could see that the crime scene was actually around the next corner; the barrier was positioned so that even if someone peaked around that first corner, they still wouldn't see anything.

"Good thinking," he muttered.

As he approached the next corner, he could hear the snapping of the cameras and the quiet chatter of the forensics team going over the scene. He rounded the corner and then paused. Breegan liked to take in the whole scene before digging into the details. Details without the bigger picture could easily lead to false interpretations. After all his years with the force, he was wary of jumping to conclusions, so he scanned the tableau before him. The body lay in the corner nearest the service elevators. Did the murderer trap the victim in this dead end?

Was the victim trying to escape the murderer through the elevators? The questions began to flow through his mind.

"Whose vomit?" asked Breegan, pointing to a fragrant blue puddle.

"Detective Breegan, hi," said a florid-faced, chubby young man. "One of the two women who found the body. Apparently not used to seeing this sort of thing." A wry smile broke out on his face.

"What've we got, Steve?" asked Breegan. He pulled a notepad from his pocket and flipped it open, clicking the button on a pen in his other hand.

"32-year-old male, Karl Erkins, according to his driver's license. He doesn't appear to be missing anything from his wallet, still wearing his fancy watch. Death caused by a hole through his chest, about three inches in diameter, like a giant spear or something. Never seen anything like it." Steve spoke in the clipped sentences of a professional, one who had seen many bodies lying in out of the way corners all over town.

"Three inches?" said Breegan, incredulously. "That's one helluva weapon. Where's all the blood? Where's the splatter?" They walked toward the body as they spoke. Breegan decided the hotel's no smoking policy didn't apply to him and dug into his pockets for another cigarette. He pulled out his pack. Holding it in one hand, he thumped it against his other hand with a practiced movement, causing a cigarette to jump part way out of the pack. He put the end in his mouth and pulled it the rest of the way.

"That's the interesting part," said Steve. The younger cop had a way of thinking of murder as an interesting puzzle, an impersonal event, though Breegan was pretty sure the victims took it personally. Breegan could do the job, could set aside emotions while working the case, but he never forgot that each case left gaping holes in the lives of real people. "There just isn't much blood left," Steve continued. "Not as much as you would expect from a wound that size. And there's very little splatter on the wall. I don't think it was any kind of gun."

"Right. One of these crazy costumed freaks killed him with a spear. Is that what you're suggesting?" He squatted next to the body and peered into the hole. He lit his cigarette absentmindedly and took a long pull.

"Maybe," said Steve. "But no costume spear could do that. And the force needed to make a hole like that…it's almost like an industrial press. This is the kind of thing you see in a car wreck where someone drives into a pole at seventy."

"Yeah," said Breegan. "Only this ain't a car wreck, is it?" He looked over the body and the questions multiplied. The corpse was strangely peaceful, except for the gaping wound. No signs of struggle, no other damage to the body, and most of the blood gone. The victim hadn't been robbed, he had just been skewered and then put down almost gently. The only other sign of violence at the scene was the broken cell phone next to the body, apparently dropped during the murder.

"Have you determined a time of death?" Breegan asked, looking up at Steve through his smoke cloud.

"One of the women called 9-1-1 at 10:02 AM. It appears that they came on the scene right after it happened. They said the blood was still dripping and the victim appeared to be drooling."

"The girls that found him, what else did they tell you? Did they see anything?" Breegan rubbed his face, a not-hopeful feeling was settling in his belly. This case was starting off strange and seemed to be getting stranger.

"They were pretty wasted," Steve said. "And shook up."

"Wasted? At ten in the morning?"

Steve shrugged. "It's the convention. Almost *everybody's* wasted. But, anyway, they say they ran into a *demon*," Steve emphasized the word, "coming around the last corner down the hall. They described him as over six feet tall, extremely muscular, with a single horn coming out of his forehead." Steve and Breegan looked at each other, both sets of eyebrows raising ever so slightly.

"A single horn. From his forehead." The feeling in Breegan's belly became worrisome and decided it was there for the duration. "Someone in a demon costume? That would be some costume to do this. Maybe we need to question the girls again after they sober up. And separately, too. Where are they now?"

Steve pulled at his sleeve, a nervous habit of his. "They're at County General. Psych Ward. They were pretty shaken up. The docs have them sedated. It might be a day or two before they are lucid again."

"Shit," said Breegan. "A day or two is too long. We need to talk to them again before that. See what you can do."

Steve nodded and pulled a cell phone out of his pocket. He turned to one side, tapped on the screen a few times, and then held the device to his ear.

Breegan crushed his cigarette on the floor and barked at the forensics team, "Alright, people. Let's wrap this up here. Get the body to the morgue and see if it can tell us anything more. I want this area roped off until further notice."

Chapter Three

B REEGAN HEADED TO THE front of the hotel, looking for the manager. As he got closer to the main lobby, the number of people grew exponentially. Soon Breegan was shuffling through an almost solid mass of bodies, the vast majority in costumes. Not being familiar with science fiction or fantasy themes, he didn't realize what the majority of characters were supposed to be, though here and there he saw a Superman or a Spiderman and he recognized witches and mummies. There were many weapons in the lobby, all props he hoped, but you never knew. *These people are crazy*, he thought, *there's no telling what some nut job has brought here.*

Breegan picked his way through the crowds, moving from one open patch of floor to another, his progress alternating between a slow, shuffling, zombie-like gait to a near trot where the crowd thinned. He was coming close to the main entrance when he noticed that the officer that had escorted him to the crime scene was waving at him, trying to get his attention. *This doesn't look good*, Breegan thought. He frowned and pushed his way through the crowd.

"What is it, Officer?" he asked as he finally reached the man.

"Sir, you need to come with me." The officer wore a grim look, darker than the one Breegan had seen earlier.

Breegan waved a hand and said, "Lead the way." They began to thread their way back across the lobby. Normally the uniform had the effect of parting crowds, but with everyone in costume, no one took the officer seriously. So they continued to weave through the throng, making slow progress. Eventually, they moved out of the lobby and down one of the less crowded hallways.

"Where are we going?" asked Breegan.

"The basement, sir." The officer was tight-lipped, clearly not interested in speaking, either about where they were going or just making small talk. That was all right with Breegan. He was in no mood for small talk, either.

They walked up to a door that read "Authorized Personnel Only." It opened upon a stairwell clearly not intended for guests. The officer led the way down the stairs, their shoes crunching lightly on the gritty dust. The stairwell was cooler than the rest of the hotel and felt damp to Breegan. They wound their way down three stories and exited the stairs through another door that opened into the basement. From the door, Breegan could see a small crowd of blue uniforms milling around an area down the hallway. He dug in his pocket and pulled out his phone. He punched the speed dial number for Steve and put the phone to his ear as they walked toward the uniforms.

"Steve? Yeah. Get down to the basement. Bring the rest of the team. I think we've got something else to look at." He hung up the phone and returned it to his pocket. He continued rummaging in his coat and pulled out his pack of cigarettes. Again he thumped the pack and a cigarette jumped. As he thrust it into his mouth and flicked his lighter, the officer said, "Sir, you can't—" Breegan shot a look at the beat cop that made him forget the rest of his sentence. He lit the cigarette and thoughtfully inhaled.

"Are you needed down here, Officer?" he asked with an edge of menace in his voice. "Why don't you go find the hotel manager and bring him here?" The officer didn't reply but turned and quickly headed back to the stairs. Breegan snorted and continued down the hall. He flashed his badge at another officer who was guarding the scene.

"What's going on here," he asked. It wasn't yet noon, but he felt as though he had already put in a full shift.

"Two bodies, sir. Maintenance men from the hotel. I've never seen anything like it, sir," said the officer, clearly shaken.

"Let me guess. Big holes. No blood." Breegan grinned, which made the officer take half a step back. Breegan's grin faded as he walked further into the scene and realized that he was not, in fact, joking.

The scene was surreal. One wall of the hall was broken open in a large hole that look like an explosion had taken place behind the wall. But there was no cavern behind the wall, just a solid wall of rock. The rubble from the wall lay scattered around the hall as though blown outward from the wall. Lying in the debris were two bodies dressed in light grey jumpsuits with the hotel logo over the right pocket. In the center of the chests of both men was a large hole, about three inches in diameter. There was very little blood.

Breegan squatted beside one of the bodies and looked into the wound. It went completely through the body. He sat back on his heels and exhaled. A patch on the corpse's jumpsuit read "Bob" over the left pocket. He gazed at the man's face, the eyes open wide, a surprised look still on the pale face.

"Not a good day, eh, Bob?" he sighed.

Steve and the rest of the forensic team came down the hall at a rapid shuffle, dragging their equipment behind.

"What do we have?" panted Steve. He was slightly overweight and had apparently run down the stairs, judging by his flushed complexion and sweaty brow.

"Take a look," said Breegan. "Seem familiar?" He stood up and stretched his back while Steve quickly examined the scene.

"Oh, jeez!" said Steve. "This is exactly the same!" He let out a whistle and ran a hand through his hair. "This is pretty serious," he said, as though a single murder were nothing to get excited about. "This is a serial killer."

"Hold on, now," said Breegan, "Let's not start throwing that word around. But, yeah, I think it's safe to say these murders were committed by the same person. Let's get to work."

The team spread out their gear and fell into the routine of gathering data from the scene. The camera flashed and the trail of objects was mapped out. Steve studied the pattern the debris made and shook his head.

"I don't understand this," he said. "This was a solid cinderblock wall, it didn't just fall down. These blocks were thrown from the wall with a great deal of force, but there's absolutely no sign of anything that could've done that, no sign of something pushing on them. Except, of course, for the fact that they're scattered all over like this." He gestured in a wide arc. The rubble was spread over a considerable distance, large chunks of masonry and small, all covered in a gritty dust. The wall opposite the opening showed damage from being hit by the fragments.

"So these two came down here to look at this hole and met the killer. Do you think the tremor this morning did this?" asked Breegan.

"This doesn't look like earthquake damage to me. I would expect a quake to cause a collapse, not an ejection like this. Besides, look at the rock behind the breach. It doesn't look damaged at all."

Breegan saw the officer escorting a man in a suit down the hall. "Keep at it, Steve. I'll find out what this guy knows." He finished his cigarette and walked toward the manager. He stuck out his hand and said, "I'm Detective Breegan. You must be the hotel manager. I need to ask you a few questions."

The manager shook hands and said, "Yes, I'm Joe Stern. I'm the manager. I gave a statement already about the man upstairs. I'm—oh my God!" He was staring past Breegan at the bodies in the rubble. "This is horrible. I've never...we've never. Nothing like this has ever happened at the hotel before." He was trembling and beginning to sweat.

"I would think not," said Breegan. "I have almost twenty years on the force and I've never seen anything quite like this. What can you tell me about these two?" He pulled out his notebook, opened it, and poised a pen over the page.

"The older one is Pete Simon. He's the—I mean, he was the maintenance supervisor. The other one is Bob Brand, one of the night maintenance men." Joe pulled at his fingers and couldn't take his eyes from the horrific view before him. He loosened his tie and undid his collar button.

"Can you tell me why they were down here? Do you have any idea when they came down here?" Breegan asked.

"I'm not sure, to be honest. It must've been right around shift change this morning. Bob never stays late after his shift. The power went out for a while right around that time. Maybe they came down to look at that." He pointed to the electrical equipment nearby and said, "This is the main power distribution point for the hotel."

"I see," said Breegan. "Was there any damage reported from the tremor this morning?"

"No, thankfully we don't seem to have any damage. Other than this wall, I guess." He shook his head. "Bob has two young children at home," his voice trailed off.

"Have you had any trouble in the hotel recently? Can you think of anyone who would do this?"

"No, besides the occasional guest who has too much to drink in the bar, the hotel is very quiet. I'm not aware of any trouble with the maintenance staff, either. I just don't know what to say about this."

"Well, let's not say anything for now," warned Breegan. "We don't need word of this to get around until we know a little more about what's going on."

Joe nodded his head enthusiastically. He thought of the convention and what would happen to his guest list if the word got out. "No, problem detective. I won't say a word. Not even to my wife."

"Good. That's all for now. I'll be in touch." They shook hands again and Joe walked toward the stairs, glancing back over his shoulder a few times, and shaking his head sadly.

Breegan walked over to the electrical equipment and looked it over. There was a little minor damage to the side facing the hole in the wall—scrapes in the paint apparently caused by the ejected cinderblocks— but nothing that would disrupt the power. There was no damage to the conduit leading to and from the huge box.

Steve walked over. "See something?" he asked.

"No, not really," Breegan said. "That's the problem. The hotel manager said the power went out this morning around the time of the tremor, which was also right around shift change for these mainte- nance guys. But you can see this equipment hasn't been damaged. So why did the power go out? A disruption in the power grid for this part of the city?"

"I hadn't heard of any, but I'll check," said Steve, making a note. "Ready to hear about these guys?"

"Yeah, give it to me."

"The wounds are the same as the victim upstairs. A three inch hole and most of the blood missing. Also like the other vic, they don't appear to have been robbed. The older one has a blunt force injury to the head. I would say he was knocked down while the perp did the younger one and then he got his chest wound, too."

"Well, this has been quite a day, hasn't it?" asked Breegan. He flipped through his notepad, checking his facts, and trying to make sense of the morning's events. "We've got our work cut out for us, don't we? What do you say we get some lunch and see if we can make heads or tails of this?" He snapped the notepad shut and thrust it into a pocket. After almost twenty years, Breegan didn't lose his appetite over a couple of bodies.

"Ok, sounds good. I'm starving," said Steve. Breegan had never known Steve to lose his appetite, either.

Chapter Four

THE MAIN SECTION OF the hotel was built around a grand lobby, with two mezzanines towering above it. But as high as the mezzanines stood above the lobby floor, they, too, were dwarfed by the towering canyon of space above them. The open space soared up from the lobby to skylights on the roof forty stories above. Half a dozen glass elevators rode on tracks that clung to the walls, giving the guests a stomach-turning view as they were whisked from the lobby to their floor at a breakneck pace. Riding the elevator down to the lobby was almost like free-falling. Guests with weak stomachs were cautioned to face the door at all times.

Breegan and Steve sat in a booth at the rear of a restaurant on the second mezzanine, looking over their menus and quietly making small talk. Darkly paneled with thick carpeting and curious, shaggy modern art tapestries hanging on the walls, the restaurant offered a respite from the noise of the convention and their booth, a semi-private place to talk. Despite the air conditioning, their goblets of ice water were sweating profusely onto the tabletop. After the waiter took their orders and left, their conversation turned toward the case at hand.

"Alright, Steve," started Breegan, "what are your thoughts?"

"Well," said Steve, "this is a new one for me." He laid his clipboard on the table and leafed through the pages of notes. He shook his head and said, "I'm not even sure where to start. So much of this makes no sense."

Breegan nodded and dug in his pocket for his notepad. "At least the timeline seems fairly clear," he said, consulting his notes. "The power went out around six, and our two maintenance men go to the basement to check on it. They have a fatal encounter instead. About four hours later, Mr....uh..." he paused to flip through notes, "... Erkins has the same encounter, and our perp is apparently ID'd by two drunk partiers. A demon.

With a horn." Again their eyes met and eyebrows arched.

"Well, a demon is nothing in this crowd," said Steve. "I saw a handful of Ewoks just walking to this restaurant. So, yes, the perp could well be walking around dressed up as a demon. What I find fascinating is the wound. I mean, how did the perp do that?" He was gesturing wildly now despite the water glass in his hand. Water slopped onto the table top as he continued. "What kind of weapon could make that sort of hole...with no blood spatter? Amazing!"

Steve took academic detachment to a whole new level, thought Breegan. They had worked together for years, and Steve had always had that attitude, but it still disturbed Breegan a little. As jaded as he had become over his many years on the force, he could still see the human factor, while Steve seemed to be almost entirely oblivious to it.

"Right," said Breegan. "And what's the motive? Not robbery. Just random murder?" He frowned and gazed across the restaurant at the innocent, unsuspecting people enjoying their meals. He fiddled with his fork and thought that people really were better off not knowing some of the things that went on in this world. He took a long drink of ice water and settled back in the booth.

They sat in silence for a few minutes, each lost in his own thoughts. The puzzle was incomplete, the pieces they had seemed to fit together but didn't tell them much. They knew what happened, but not how or why. And most importantly, they didn't know who the murderer was or where that person was right now. Or what they were doing.

"And what about all the—" Steve stopped himself as the waiter brought their meals. He played with his napkin while he waited for the man to leave and then resumed. "What about all the blood? What happened to the blood? Would you pass me the ketchup?"

Breegan passed the bottle and shook his head. "Dunno," he mumbled around a bite of medium rare steak. "It certainly is quite a trick." He chewed thoughtfully and considered the possibilities. He pointed at Steve with his fork and said, "Could the weapon be some kind of pipe that not only caused the wound but also drained the blood away?"

"I suppose so," Steve nodded. "But that's a gallon, maybe a gallon and a half per person. Is the killer walking around with a five-gallon can full of blood?" asked Steve. "And a big pipe with a hose attached? And some sort of pump?"

Breegan shook his head and grinned, "Does seem kinda far-fetched, doesn't it? Hand me the salt, would you?" He sprinkled his fries and continued, "So the blood question is a dead-end for now. But I have a feeling that's a key to this whole thing."

Steve took the salt back and sprinkled his food, and they lapsed into silence again. Their thoughts were accompanied by the burbling noise of the restaurant, the soft talk and occasional laughter of other guests, the random clinking of utensils on plates.

"Is there a black market for blood, do you think?" offered Steve.

"Never heard of one," said Breegan. "Body parts, organs, sure, but I've never heard of blood."

"This one's off to an interesting start," said Steve. "Lots of evidence that doesn't add up and this guy still roaming around on the loose."

"I agree, we've got plenty of nothing." Breegan stuffed his notepad and pen back into his pocket and pondered their next moves. *How do you catch the invisible man?* he thought.

The waiter returned and offered dessert, which the duo declined. Then came the ritual of the chcck, suun settled, and they walked out of the restaurant and back into the din of the convention. Back into the world of the blissfully ignorant.

"I hate to say it," said Breegan, "but we need more info. I just hope we can get it without finding another body." He cleaned his teeth with a toothpick and then used it to point around the hotel. "This guy could be anywhere. He could be right in front of us."

Steve nodded. "I'm going to head to the morgue. I want to see if they've found anything else on the bodies. Call me if you need me."

Chapter Five

O FFICER PERKINS SHIFTED HIS
weight back and forth from one foot to the
other. Too bad he couldn't find a chair to sit on.
Guarding a crime scene was one of the most
tedious duties for the average beat cop. Especially
this scene, deep in the basement of a hotel, nothing
really to look at, no sunlight, not even a breeze to
relieve the monotony. It seemed ridiculous to him.
This part of the basement wasn't even open to the
public, and most of the hotel staff never came to
this out of the way section of the hotel. Those that
might have business there had been warned to stay
away. There was almost no chance of anyone stumbling upon the scene and disturbing any evidence
that hadn't yet been collected. But procedure was
procedure, and Detective Breegan had left specific

orders that the scene was to be secured at all times. Disobeying Breegan wasn't an idea that Perkins relished—the man had a reputation. So he alternated between shifting his weight back and forth and pacing the hallway from the scene to the stairwell and back. Whistling helped drown out the eerie silence of the basement, too.

Perkins guarded the scene for what seemed like an eternity. He counted the number of times he made a lap of the area but lost count somewhere after forty two. He whistled every tune he knew and then spent some time just whistling randomly. Nothing he made up sounded very good to him, so he stopped. He began to wonder if Central had forgotten to send him a relief. Perkins didn't wear a watch or carry a cell phone, so he had no way of checking the time. Surely it was the middle of the night by now. In reality, only three-quarters of an hour had passed when another officer took his place just long enough for him to use the restroom and grab a quick bite for lunch. The necessities of life had to fit around the duties of a working policeman.

When he returned to the basement hall, he quickly settled back into his routine, shifting and pacing and whistling. He thought wistfully of his father's pig farm in South Georgia and wondered if the life of a pig farmer would be more exciting than this. You had to put up with the smell, he knew, but you got to move around more and be out in the sunlight. He sighed and started pacing again.

A noise caught his ear and attention. He paused his pacing and listened but decided he didn't hear anything. "Must be imagining things," he said to himself and began shifting his weight back and forth. The boredom could cause your brain to invent things, he knew, so he started to make a mental list of the pros and cons of being a pig farmer. "I could probably wear a cowboy hat," he thought.

He heard the noise again. He paused and held his breath to listen more carefully. This time he was sure he heard a sound. A faint crackling, a slight buzzing, like the sound static electricity makes when you take off a sweater, just before you shock yourself. The sound was growing louder, on the air the faint odor of ozone. The floor seemed to vibrate, and Perkins wondered if his lunch was bothering him.

He turned to look in the direction of the noise. It was coming from the opening in the wall. A cold breeze began to emanate from the cavity, and blue lighting began to flicker around the edges. The crackling grew louder and louder, the breeze grew stronger and stronger, and the blue lightning increased in intensity and brightness. The vibration in the floor developed into a definite trembling and then outright shaking, and he could see some of the smaller bits of rubble starting to dance and jump on the ground.

Now the lightning had white streaks at the center of the veins, and its violent, swirling mass practically filled the opening in the wall. Arthritic fingers of lightning reached out toward the electrical switch block, which began to send its own white fingers toward the blue. Perkins could feel the hair on his arms and the back of his neck begin to stand on end.

A blast of cold air knocked Perkins' hat from his head and sent it skittering down the hall, his uniform flapping against his body. He had to lean into the wind as he staggered to keep his footing. It threatened to snatch the breath out of his lungs. The noise was deafening, and as he watched, the fingers of lightning from the wall met with the fingers emanating from the switch block. When they joined, there was a blinding flash and a thunderous bang, and Perkins was knocked to the ground.

The hall was plunged into darkness. The emergency lighting flickered on for the second time that day.

Perkins lay in the darkness, his body still being washed over by the torrent of cold wind gushing from the gap in the wall. As he scrambled to his feet, he pulled his flashlight from his belt and snapped on the beam. It augmented the weak emergency lighting but only in its narrow, dusty cone. The air was heavy with a fine dust, and Perkins coughed a little as he tried to catch his breath. He swung the beam toward the rift in the wall, over the electrical equipment, and up and down the hall. He saw nothing that hadn't been there before, though the opening in the wall still danced with blue lightning. It was quickly growing fainter and shrinking toward the edges of the hole. The snapping and buzzing were subsiding as well.

The wind began to ebb, and soon the hallway had reverted to its former condition, though darker now. The fine dust that filled the air began to settle on everything. Perkins brushed off and straightened his uniform and ran a hand through his hair.

"What the hell was that?" Perkins muttered. He continued to scan the area with his flashlight and settled on the electrical box. He could see that the breaker had been tripped, though he could see no other damage to the box. He reached out to reset it. He shoved the large breaker lever back on, with a grunt from him and a deep clunk from the breaker, and the box began humming again. The hallway lighting was restored, and once again the emergency lights blinked out.

Perkins switched off his flashlight and returned it to his belt. He moved carefully through the rubble toward the gape in the wall and looked inside. The hole seemed to be filled with an inky blankness. Not black, not something you could see, but a void that seemed to absorb the light and not let any back out.

Perkins' heart rate and breathing had been coming back to normal, but the strangeness of the abyss caused them to have second thoughts about settling down. Pig farming didn't have any lightless, inky voids, he was pretty sure about that.

As he peered into the fissure, he was startled as something silver winked back at him. His left hand went instinctively to the grip of the weapon on his hip, and he took a slight step backward.

The silver thing swung in a smooth arc. It seemed to be coming closer, bobbing slightly as it approached. It made a snicking sound and burst into a small flame. Perkins gripped the gun tightly, and he began to draw the weapon from its holster. His finger slid onto the trigger as his breathing and heart rate committed themselves to a serious pace.

In the small space illuminated by the flame, he could see the face of a woman lighting a cigarette in her mouth. She took a long pull on the cigarette, and the cherry ember flared brightly. As she stepped from the inky void, she exhaled a giant cloud of bluish smoke and said,"Take it easy, Junior. There's no need to get excited."

Chapter Six

AFTER STEVE LEFT, BREEGAN once again headed toward the front door of the hotel. His mind reeled with the possibilities of the case, the pieces swirling in his psyche, trying to fit together but not quite able to do so. As he threaded his way through the crowd, part of his mind wrestled with the crime, part navigated the floor, and yet another part observed the crowd around him. Three characters that might have come straight from a performance of the musical Cats were followed closely by a group of beautiful young girls who seemed to be in a competition to see which one of them could wear the least amount of clothing without being arrested. The circuses of Las Vegas surely had nothing to compare with this. Except for the adult shows, of course.

He was midway across the lobby when he noticed the lights flicker briefly off and then on again. Most people didn't notice. After all, it was early afternoon, and the ample windows and skylights of the hotel flooded the lobby with light. But Breegan noticed and stopped dead in his tracks. He had a sinking feeling in his stomach. He resumed his trek to the outside world. He was only thirty yards from the door. On an average day, he would have covered that distance in a matter of seconds, but with the throng of the convention surrounding him, his progress was much slower.

He had nearly reached the entrance when the sinking feeling was reinforced by the vibration radiating from the pocket that held his cell phone. He stopped again and reluctantly dug it out of his pocket. He looked at the screen. "Damn," he swore, softly. "The dispatcher." He stabbed the screen and put the phone to his ear.

"Breegan. What is it?" The voice murmured its official patter in his ear. "Right. I'm on it." He stabbed the screen again and stuffed the phone back into his pocket. "Damn," he swore again and turned to head toward the basement once more. *This is turning into one helluva day*, he thought.

Breegan tried to hurry through the crowd, but

the crowd was having no part of it. He pulled out his badge and waved it around. No one paid him any attention. He pulled out his gun with the other hand and waved that, too. Still, no one noticed. "Damn," he swore yet again and shoved the badge and gun back into the nether regions of his clothing. *This convention is a pain in my ass*, he thought. *Is there no respect for authority?*

At length, he broke free of the crowd and started down the hallway to the service stairs to the basement. He was joined by several uniformed policemen. Apparently, the dispatcher had been feeling zealous. They recognized him and respectfully fell into a loose jumble behind him. He shoved open the door, and as the detective headed down the three stories to the basement, followed by the thudding steps of a half dozen patrolmen, a weariness settled around him that made him wish for a tall bourbon and a warm, soft bed.

Round and round they went, spiraling their way down the stairwell to the basement. Breegan felt as though the stairs were an old, familiar acquaintance as his hand slid along the railing and his feet shuffled wearily over the treads. The sound of the grit under his feet was a familiar song, too, and for some inexplicable reason, he found himself thinking about pig farming.

He burst through the basement door with his entourage of men in blue in tow and strode purposefully toward the mysterious break in the wall. As Breegan approached, he could see another uniformed cop crouched with sidearm drawn, the weapon aimed at a curious figure in front of him. Breegan's stride slowed as he neared, trying to take in the scene.

The cop was obviously nervous, visibly trembling as he kept the woman in his sights, sweat in beads on his forehead. The woman stood calmly smoking, seemingly paying no attention to the policeman. She was tall and thin, with dark, shoulder-length hair flowing out under a gray fedora. One hand held the cigarette she puffed industriously while the other hand was tucked into the belt of her long tan trench coat, jauntily tied, not buckled, around her waist. She looked for all the world like a female Humphrey Bogart, stepped straight out of a transgender Casablanca.

"What's going on here, Officer? What's your name? Are you new in this precinct?" asked Breegan. The woman's cigarette looked appealing, so he dug into his own pockets and performed his ritual smack, grab and light.

"P-Perkins, sir. Yes, I've only b-been in this p-precinct a couple of weeks now. I've...uh...appre-hended this wuh-wuh-oman," he stuttered.

Breegan held up both hands in the universal "whoa there" sign, the cigarette dangling from his mouth dancing up and down as he spoke. "Ok, Perkins. Let's just relax a little. She doesn't seem to be very threatening, does she?" As he said this, the woman shot him a look under the brim of her fedora that made Breegan question his last statement.

Perkins visibly relaxed a little, standing up a little straighter, and lowering his weapon slightly.

"So, Perkins," Breegan continued, "what's going on here?"

"Well, sir, I was guarding the scene, see, and she just...well...there was this noise. And a wind. And lights! And I lost my hat, and then she just appeared!" he said in a rush.

"Just appeared. From where?" Breegan asked.

"Well, from there," said the policeman, pointing at the solid rock exposed by the breach in the wall.

"Uh huh. From there, was it?" Breegan's eyebrow was beginning to cramp from being raised so often in one day. "How long have you been on duty today, Perkins?" he asked.

Before Perkins could reply, the woman looked directly at Breegan, took a step forward, and asked, "Are you in charge?" As she did so, Perkins instantly resumed his crouching stance and snapped his weapon back to aim at her chest.

"Whoa, Officer Perkins," said Breegan. "I think I can take it from here. Why don't you head upstairs and get a…" He wanted to say, "drink," but then realized that that was not quite appropriate given the time of day and the duty status of the officer in question. He paused and finished awkwardly, "take a break."

Perkins hesitated and looked anxiously between Breegan and the woman. Something convinced him of the appropriateness of getting a…taking a break…and he gradually stood up, holstered his weapon, and walked slowly away from the scene. Thoughts of happy pigs playing in the sunlight danced through his head.

The other officers milled nervously as Breegan stepped forward. "So, Miss…do you have a name?" he asked.

"My name is Sammu-Ramat Spade," she said,

rolling the R with a clipped British accent.. "You can call me Sam." She stepped closer to him.

"Sam," he said, with a twist of irony in his voice. "Sam…Spade. You want me to call you Sam Spade?"

"Of course," she said. "That is my name."

One eyebrow arched high over Breegan's eye. The day was clearly not done messing with his head. He drew in on his cigarette and blew out pensively. "What are you doing here," he paused, "Sam?"

"I'm here on assignment," she said, quickly looking around the hall. "Where are the bodies," she asked.

Breegan paused and looked at her. He took a last long drag on his cigarette and then pulled it from his mouth, nestled between two fingers of his right hand, and scratched his lower lip with the thumb of that hand. He held his breath for a moment and then exhaled slowly, purposefully, tossing the butt down and crushing it under his foot. He cocked an eyebrow at her again and said, "What bodies?"

She seemed not to notice his hesitation. "The two bodies that were lying here," she said impatiently as she waved a hand to indicate the former location of the murdered maintenance men. "Two men. And their discarded flashlights, if I'm seeing things correctly." She turned to face him. She took a puff on her cigarette as they locked eyes.

"I'm not sure I'm following you," said Breegan, as the hair stood up on the back of his neck and a chill ran down his back. The bodies had been removed and there were no tape marks on the debris-strewn ground. And the flashlights, now safely bagged and tagged and stored in the Evidence Room, how on Earth could she know they had been lying there, too?

"For Pete's sake, man! Let's not beat around the bush! Big holes. Very little blood. Does that not ring a bell?" she asked incredulously.

Chapter Seven

BREEGAN RAN HIS HAND through his hair. *How many times will I do this today*, he wondered. Seeing that it was still early afternoon and he had already had the most interesting, puzzling day of his life, he wasn't sure of the answer to that question. Lost in thought, his hand rummaged for his pack of cigarettes and pulled it out, only to be disappointed because it was empty. Out before evening. *This is some kind of day*, he thought. Sam Spade dug a pack out of a pocket in her tan trench coat and offered him one.

"Thanks," he said weakly. He stuck the Chesterfield in his mouth and lit it. He took a long drag and slowly blew out a giant cloud of bluish smoke. It didn't make him feel any better.

He and Sam had moved to the ground floor

maintenance office to talk, a small cloud of uniforms stood outside the door, just in case. He looked her over. Grey fedora, tan trench coat, high-waisted slacks and a short, fat tie. *She is straight out of the forties*, he thought. *Straight out of a Bogie movie*, he continued as his hand wandered to the back of his neck and rubbed.

Sam Spade, indeed, he thought. *Could the day get any stranger*, he wondered. *No, don't think that*, he scolded himself. *Don't give it an idea!*

"So…Sam. You were wandering in the base-ment and startled our young Officer Perkins. What were you doing in that part of the hotel?" he asked, notepad open and pen poised.

"I wasn't wandering. I came through the portal after the demon. I've been sent to bring him back. He's busted out of jail, don'tcha see?" She was earnest, but there was something peculiar about her speech.

"Portal?" Breegan echoed. "Jail?" *You think you've seen it all*, he thought, *think you've heard it all. Maybe I need a vacation.* His thoughts drifted off and found nowhere comfortable to settle.

"Yes, jail," Sam said. Inpatient and annoyed, she shot Breegan a look that left little doubt as to her state of mind. "You do understand the concept of "jail" here, don't you?"

"There's no need to get mouthy, Miss. Of course I understand the word "jail." It's the word "portal" that's giving me trouble." He was annoyed, too, but the bizarreness of the day had overpowered him to the point where his annoyance was just a minor, nagging issue, barely enough to come to the forefront of his mind.

"Ah. I see," she said as if something was suddenly settled in her mind. "What year is this?" she asked.

"Year?" he echoed. The ripples of confusion in his mind had long since grown into tidal waves. "It's 2018, of course," he said with little surprise in his voice. Of course it was, he reassured himself.

"Yes. 2018. That makes sense now," she said with finality. Breegan was glad that it made sense to someone.

"Portals make sense in 2018," he said, as though he were trying to convince himself of that particular brand of logic.

"Listen…say, what's your name, Mac?" she asked. She looked at him as though she were seeing him for the first time. He felt hopeful because this was the first question of the afternoon to which he felt reasonably sure he knew the answer.

"Breegan," he said hopefully. "Connor Breegan." He smiled, a weak feeling of triumph settling on him. That much he knew.

"Ok, Breegan Connor Breegan, listen carefully —" she began, but he interrupted her.

"No, just "Breegan" is fine," he corrected. For once, since she had started talking, he felt like he had the upper hand. At least partially.

"Ok, Breegan," she continued, "here's the deal. I'm a cop, too. I'm from the TransDimensional Police Department." She flashed a badge, a dull silver chunk of metal, angular and sleek, like the lines of a jet fighter. "You probably haven't heard of us, since we're technically from another dimension. And time, now that I think about it. But never mind that," she pushed on. "The point is, we're on the same side, you just don't realize that yet, old boy." She smiled at this pause as if a simple facial expression would explain everything to Breegan. It didn't.

He continued to look doubtful as she pressed on with her explanation. "The demon…his name is Janx Wiley-Jarlett, actually…was sentenced to transdimensional prison during the last century… uh, my time that is, not yours…for attempting to overthrow the Universal Monarchy. A bit of a naughty boy!" she chuckled, thoroughly enjoying some joke.

"Wiley-Jarlett?" he asked. This did not strike him as a particularly demonic name.

"Yes, of the Outer-Tethys Jarletts. His Mother's side of the family, actually. His father was an obscure helium trader who made a name for himself when he stole the third moon of Uranus and sold it on the black market." She chuckled again and shook her head, as though remembering a nephew's cheeky prank. "In any event, Janx plotted to overthrow the Monarchy, as I said. Quite a few dignitaries were killed, as a matter of fact, before he was captured, along with the rest of his followers. All of them were sentenced to life in transdimensional prison, which should have been the end of it." She frowned and looked annoyed.

Breegan was scribbling furiously in his notepad, his mind not quite digesting everything he was hearing. "Outer-Tethys," he mumbled. "Transdimensional."

"Yes, transdimensional. It's the most secure type of prison, really. Very tricky to break out of. In fact, no one has ever managed it before now." She smiled again. "But, by some thick slice of luck, Janx somehow managed to come through a portal into this particular dimension. Not sure how. The boffins were muttering something about the alignment of certain planets and your Sun generating some sort of transdimensional earthquake. Or something like that. I never can quite understand the boffins, you know!" she quipped, apparently again enjoying a private joke.

"Transdimensional earthquake? We did have a tremor here this morning," said Breegan, who finally felt as though he might be beginning to regain his footing.

"Well that would be the one, now, wouldn't it?" she asked, though it didn't seem like a question to Breegan. "And, of course, what with his strength, combined with that nasty horn and his thirst for blood, he made short work of those two men, didn't he? What were they doing down there, anyway?" she asked, her fount of wisdom somewhat dry in this area.

"They were maintenance men, down there to restore the power after the quake," he said. "What do you mean, "thirst for blood"?" Like a tennis match, it was Breegan's turn to ask a question again.

"He's a Joob. Fascinating race, really. They

require blood as their primary form of nourishment. In prison, they're given a synthetic substitute. I'm sure he was excited to have the real thing again." She smiled grimly this time, suddenly taking the topic very seriously. "Let's just hope we can find him before he finds another victim. He'll want to feed every few hours."

"We're a little late for that," Breegan said. "He found another victim after he killed the first two." His mind quickly did the arithmetic and knew that feeding time was growing near, if not already past.

"Ah, I see," she said. "When was that, exactly?"

"Well, about two hours ago," he said slowly. They exchanged knowing looks and consulted their watches. "So, it's just about time for another—" he started.

"Yes, well that would fit with his physiological needs, that's for certain." She looked grim but calm. "So what is your plan, Mr. Breegan?" She look him in the eye, as though sizing him up, and waited attentively for his response.

"My plan?" he responded. To be honest, a plan for catching a serial killer with no clear motive was shaky at best. If he were truly to consider the murderer to be a transdimensional alien, well, that was out of his realm of experience. His shaky plan just became nonexistent. "Normally I would have to wait until some sort of motive became apparent. From there I could establish a pattern of behavior and, hopefully, predict the killer's next moves. Then we could try to get ahead of him...." His words trailed off, as if he realized the weakness of this plan.

"Wait?" she said. She paused, letting the implication sink into the conversation. "He will try to feed every couple of hours, Breegan. How long do you propose to wait?" She couldn't keep the testiness out of her voice. In fact, it never occurred to her to try to keep it out.

Breegan was one of the most respected detectives on the force, and he was getting tired of feeling like a green beat cop. "First of all, you actually expect me to believe all this? A transdimensional fugitive? A portal through space-time? That your name is Sam Spade? I should throw you in jail until you start making more sense." Finally, he felt as though he could put his elevated heart rate to good use. A little old fashioned yelling might just do the trick.

"Well, to be honest," she said, my name isn't really Spade. We don't have last names where I come from. I did some research into your dimension before I crossed the portal, to just, you know, fit in better. These clothes, the name. My research seemed to show that this is how detectives appear in this dimension. Is this not correct?" she asked.

"Maybe for a Hollywood detective in the nineteen forties!" he said, smiling with actual happiness for what seemed like the first time in ages. "But that still doesn't explain all this talk about transdimensional portals and Universal Monarchies. How am I supposed to believe all this?"

"Tell me, detective, besides the terminology that is giving you a little difficulty, which parts don't fit with what you know? The part where this "demon" can cause a gaping wound but leaves little blood behind? The part where the place from whence the "demon" appeared looks like an explosion from nowhere? Perhaps it's the electrical storm that disrupts your power grid but doesn't damage it?" She glared at him now. But it was a glare that was concerned with his unwillingness to see the facts, not a glare of anger at his person. She was concerned that he refused to see what his eyes saw, refused to put the pieces together, even though he subconsciously saw how they fit.

"You know," she continued, "he is hyper-intelligent. He has probably already learned your language. It only took me a couple of hours, after all. He is able to fit in here now as though he were a native. We're just lucky his appearance will stand out...what's the expression? Like a wounded thumb?"

"Uh, well, about that..." his voice trailed off. "There's something I should show you."

Chapter Eight

THEY STOOD IN THE lobby of the hotel, a vast sea of costumed people surging back and forth in front of them.

Science fiction characters, elves, witches, wizards, dwarves, robots…so many varieties of each type of character. As Breegan and Sam watched the crowd, two groups of elves ran by, one dressed mostly in green, the other mostly black. As the two groups dodged through the crowd, they pretended to shoot at each other with their long, delicate bows. The people who were dressed "normally" seem to be the oddities. Their mouths hung open in disbelief as they surveyed the scene before them. Movies and comic books had sprung to life, and their overwrought brains struggled to make sense of what they saw.

The implications were not lost on Sammu-Ramat. Her fugitive, who, by every sense of rationality, should've stuck out like the proverbial sore thumb, had chanced upon a situation where his appearance would go completely unnoticed. Or rather, not unnoticed, but unremarked. Even that didn't fit the situation correctly. If his appearance were remarked upon, it would be in appreciation of the excellent work he had done on his costume, which was no costume at all.

Sam grinned as she began to appreciate the irony. The boffins spoke of an inversion of the reality probabilities. That the improbable would become probable in this event, and that she should expect to find the unexpected. At the time, she thought it was just the usual impenetrable boffin-speak, but now she was beginning to understand what they meant.

"What in the world is this?" she asked, incredulously. "Some sort of mental institution?" She was speaking to Breegan, standing at her side, but she couldn't take her eyes from the crowd. The improbability of it all was irresistible.

"Well, not insanity. Not in the strictest, legally actionable sense of the word, anyway. These people are fans of science fiction and fantasy entertainment. You know, movies, books, comic books. Stuff like that. They just enjoy dressing up as their favorite characters," he said, shrugging his shoulders and looking slightly embarrassed for his fellow dimension-members.

"Well, obviously, you can see where this is going to be a problem," she said, crossing her arms and contemplating the crowd more seriously. "He could be right in front of us, and we might not even notice him!"

"Surely he's not going to just keep on feeding randomly," said Breegan. "Surely he's after more than that, right?" He looked expectantly at her. This was his first transdimensional case, and he felt the need for some experienced advice.

"Good point," she said. "He's brilliant, he won't just stroll around here, killing indescriminately. I think—"

Breegan held up his hand to stop her as the cell phone in his pocket went off. "Hold one," he said as he snatched the phone from his pocket, jabbed at the screen, and held it to his ear.

"Breegan. What is it? Yes….Where?…I'm on it." He pressed the screen and thrust the phone back into his pocket.

"C'mon," he said. "He's on the move!"

Breegan led the way, this time waving his gun and shouting like a madman as he ran across the lobby. This seemed to work very well, and the crowds of people parted to let them through rather easily. Soon they emerged from the hotel into the bright light of the afternoon.

"I don't understand," said Sam. "Why would he leave the shelter of this gathering of costumed individuals to roam the streets? Why would he exposed himself to such danger?"

"Look around," he said, gesturing to the crowds on the street. "The convention is being hosted at six different hotels." The costumed contingent had spilled out of the hotel and was flowing up and down the sidewalks just as they had done in the hallways inside. The sidewalks were packed with characters from science fiction stories, new and old, fantasies and fairy tales, any sort of reality that was not of the ordinary, everyday kind. Stretching off into the distance, the costumed throng clogged the sidewalks and spilled into the streets. Monsters and science fiction characters were the norm, as if comic books and movies had opened up and spilled their contents all over the streets of downtown Atlanta.

"Ah," said Sam. "I see. Is this sort of thing usual in your dimension?"

"Well, yes and no. Normal on an annual basis, yes. But otherwise, no," Breegan said as he continued to lead her down the sidewalk. His mind was still reeling from the events of the day. He began to question his own sanity. *Do I actually believe I'm leading an alien detective down the sidewalks of Atlanta? Do I really believe there is an alien demon on the loose, killing innocent people and feeding on their blood?* While section of his brain struggled with these questions, another, more functional part, follow the procedures and habits had developed over his years on the force. The answers to his first questions were immaterial. He was sure of one thing, murders had been committed, and he would capture the murderer. The dispatcher had reported another death fitting the day's MO in the hotel adjacent to the first. As they walked down the noisy sidewalk, he pulled out his cell phone and called Steve.

"Steve?" he yelled into the phone. "Bring the team. The Hyatt. We've got another one, apparently. OK. See you there." He hung up and stuffed the phone back into his pocket.

They moved down the sidewalk, Sam fitting in with the costumed revelers rather better than

Breegan did. At one point, she was even asked to pose for a photograph by another costumed couple. It seemed as though a small army of photographers had also descended on the streets of Atlanta. Impromptu photo sessions appeared at random intervals along the sidewalks. Soon they approached the next hotel on the block. A uniformed cop was waiting at the entrance to guide them.

"Detective Breegan," he said as he flashed his badge. "This is..." he started to say as he turned toward Sam. But then the ridiculousness of introducing a transdimensional policewoman dawned on him, and he simply finished with, "a colleague of mine."

"This way, sir," the officer said and turned to lead them into the hotel. They slowly wound their way through the crowded lobby and headed to one of the less inhabited side halls that led away from the throng of convention goers. The officer led them to a bathroom with another uniformed policewoman standing guard outside. "The victim is inside, sir," she said as he held the door open.

"My team is coming. Make sure they get here as soon as possible," Breegan said to the officer and headed into the restroom. The scene felt familiar to him, and in the back of his mind Breegan recorded the fact that he was jaded.

It was a typical hotel restroom. Beige marble, dark wood, and stainless steel. Potted plants occupied the corners, and there was even a red velvet couch. Breegan never understood why ladies' rooms had couches in them. The bathroom smelled of mild disinfectant and perfume. But there was another scent, as well. Breegan could make out the faint scent of blood. At the back of the ladies' room, a body sat on the floor, propped up against the wall. A person might think she was just sleeping, except for the odd choice of lodgings and the gaping hole in her chest. Her head tilted slightly to one side, a surprised look in her eyes. Besides the hole in her chest, there were surprisingly few signs of violence. Again, there was a strange lack of blood for a murder that involved perforating a body cleanly through the chest with a three-inch hole. Her purse lay on the ground beside her, undisturbed, and next to the body was a broken cell phone.

"People pick the oddest places to use their phones," said Breegan. He considered the woman on the floor and thought about how her last moments were calling someone from a public restroom. Perhaps some people just needed constant companionship, he thought. Personally, he wanted some of his personal activities to remain personal.

"Yes, yes," said Sam, somewhat excited by the scene. "This is classic! An out of the way location, the victim distracted by her conversation on her mobile, apparently. I've seen Joob feed, it's fascinating! The entire act is over in just a matter of seconds. The horn is evolved to serve not only as a stabbing weapon but also as a channel to collect the blood. What blood is missed by the horn is directed into their mouths by specialized flaps in their facial skin." She was speaking quickly and in an animated manner, with a gleam in her eyes.

"I knew it!" said Breegan. He felt some vindication for his earlier remarks to Steve in the restaurant. He was a little embarrassed by his own excitement over the death of a fellow human being, though, and tried to curb his enthusiasm. He realized, too, that he seemed to be believing in the existence of this transdimensional demon. Suddenly, he felt the need to be more restrained.

"But this really gets us nowhere, right?" he continued. "I mean, we have another body, but no further clues as to where he is now or where he's going next. This is just another pointless murder."

"Yes, you're essentially correct," said Sam. "We

have another couple of hours before he'll need to feed again. But where that will be, alas, I can't really say."

They both stood up from their crouching positions over the body. Breegan leaned against the wall, an overwhelming feeling of tiredness washing over him. He looked at Sam and pondered further whether he should believe her story. He questioned how he could ever explain this to headquarters. How could he possibly make them understand this? Or would they simply listen to his story, and quietly have him committed to the nearest asylum?

The door to the bathroom opened and Steve entered with the rest of the forensics team. As the team started to unpack their gear, Steve pulled on a pair of latex gloves. He took in the scene and let out a low whistle.

"Well, he's consistent," he said. "I'll give him that." He noticed Sam and turned to Breegan and asked, "Who's your friend?"

Breegan looked sideways at Sam and then back to Steve. His mind turned somersaults, struggling to come up with a believable explanation for his new companion. He paused, considering his options at this point. Finally, he cleared his throat and said,

"Steve, this is…a colleague of mine. Sam. Sam Spade."

Steve laughed."Sam Spade? Really? Tell me another one!" He continued laughing until he realized that neither Breegan nor Sam were joining in. Slowly his laughing subsided, his eyes darting from Breegan to Sam, expectantly. "Really," he said, "who is this?"

"Let's go into the details later, Steve," said Breegan, nervously eying the rest of the forensics team and shuffling his feet. "Sam is a colleague of mine from a….neighboring department. She has an interest in the case." He hoped this would be explanation enough for the time being.

Steve looked at Sam for another moment or two, apparently considering the wisdom of asking any further questions. Finally, he said, "OK. Fine. Let me see what we've got here."

He turned toward the body to begin sifting the clues before him. He squatted down next to the victim and carefully examined her. He gently pulled at her blouse around the wound to better view it. Just as gently, he moved her head from one side to the other looking for further signs of injury. One at a time, he lifted her hands examining the nails and, generally, tried to develop a sense of what it happened.

"The MO seems consistent. Same type of wound, distinct lack of blood. I don't think there's much doubt that this is the same killer."

Steve continued to move around the body, muttering to himself as he went. "Her purse is open," he rummaged through the bag, "but nothing seems to be missing. That fits, too. What's this? Another broken cell phone. That's fascinating." There was a slight emphasis on this last word, and a grin began to form on Steve's face. After years of working together, Breegan knew that when Steve used the word "fascinating," it was worth paying attention to.

"Why's that?" he asked.

"Well, as I'm sure you remember, the first victim…uh, in the order that we found them, that is…had a broken cell phone with him. The first two victims…chronologically speaking….didn't. The perp didn't seem to take anything from them. I mean, besides their lives. But the single man, his phone was broken, too," said Steve. He had a slight glimmer in his eye, and he knelt beside the remains of the cell phone and began to gently pick through the pieces.

"Uh, huh," said Breegan. "And why, exactly, is that so fascinating? People drop their cell phones all the time. If I were being murdered, the last thing I would be worried about is my cell phone." His voice carried a tone of annoyance, not sure what Steve was getting at. Although he was thoroughly used to Steve's ways, sometimes he couldn't help being annoyed with them.

"Just as I suspected," said Steve, ignoring Breegan's little rant. "Some of the pieces are missing," he said, triumphantly. He smiled up at Breegan, as though everything was now clear. His smile began to fade as he saw Breegan's uncomprehending look.

"Of course," said Steve. "I haven't had time to tell you. Back at the morgue, I noticed that the first victim…not chronologically speaking…oh, never mind." He frowned, then shook his head and forged ahead. "His cell phone was missing parts. The GPS module and the battery were gone!" Again he looked expectantly at Breegan.

"You're telling me the demon…the perp…is killing people to collect cell phone parts?" asked Breegan. *Perhaps there's a market for phone parts in trans-dimensional prison.* Breegan's brain no sooner had this thought than it dismissed it. A small voice in his brain began chanting, *There is no demon, there is no demon, there is no demon.* Another voice laughed at the mantra and shook its head.

"Well, no," said Steve. "Or, maybe, yes. The parts are missing. And parts are gone from this phone, too," he said, gesturing at the broken device. "This one is missing the screen and number pad. Who else would've taken them?" While he spoke, he placed the remaining cell phone parts into an evidence bag, sealed it, and wrote a description on the outside.

"That's a good question," said Breegan, scratching his head and looking perplexed. "But why?" he asked. They looked at each other, neither one venturing a guess.

"Oh, dear," said Sam. "I think I may know. And the reason I'm thinking of isn't very good news. It has to do with the transdimensional portal—"

Before she could finish, Breegan grabbed her by the elbow and propelled her out of the ladies' room.

Chapter Nine

ONCE OUTSIDE THE LADIES' room, Breegan didn't stop moving. He guided Sam gently but firmly around the corner and into the quiet alcove of a maintenance space.

"Look," he said. "I don't know where you actually come from, lady, but we need to establish some guidelines. We're dealing with factual murders here, not some fantastical, transdimensional fairytale!" Although he was trying to remain calm, the volume of his voice was rising, he could feel his heart beating faster, and heat was coming to his face. He certainly had seen some things that day that he would not have imagined yesterday, and even though part of his brain accepted what Sam was saying as the most logical... did he just say logical? ... explanation of the day's events, he knew that demons and transdimensional portals did not actually exist. He had to get to the true answer. He had to find the real murderer.

Sam looked at him softly, compassion in her eyes. She grinned slightly at him and shook her head.

"I know this is a lot for you to take in, but you really must believe me. We don't have much time to track him down and I need your help." She reached out and laid a hand on his arm as though physical contact might convey the truth of her words.

"How on earth can I believe you?" asked Breegan, his hands spread wide in the universal symbol of disbelief. There was exasperation in his tone as his mind struggled to come to grips with his thoughts.

"What do I need to do to convince you?" asked Sam. She thrust her hands deep in the pockets of her overcoat and leaned against the wall. Her right hand brushed against her badge, and immediately she knew what she had to do.

"I have it! I'll show you!" She was smiling now. "I don't know why I didn't think of this sooner, but, as they say, seeing is believing." She pulled her badge out of her pocket and held it out for him to see, lying flat in the center her outstretched palm. A look of triumph was on her face as if merely seeing the badge would clarify everything.

"What do you mean, you're going to show me?" asked Breegan, a nervous feeling suddenly gripping him. What if she was telling the truth, what if she really was from another dimension? His rational mind rejected the idea, of course, but he had seen enough this day to implant a seed of doubt in his mind, and a willingness to believe her. He involuntarily took half a step backwards and reached out to touch the wall, looking for some steadiness in his suddenly uncertain world.

"It's really quite simple," she said. "I'll just take you back to the Transdimensional Police Department, show you the prison and the remaining Joob, and it will all make sense." She smiled again as if nothing could be simpler.

While she spoke she tapped at the center of the badge, a rhythmic tap that was clearly some kind of code. The geometric design of the badge snapped open, like a mechanical flower instantly blooming under her touch. The geometric star shape of the badge had expanded, the points now going outward, revealing a smooth, black, metal disk underneath. Her fingertip played on the metal disk, first sliding one direction, tapping another rhythmic code, and sliding in the other direction. From where he stood, Breegan could see lights appear on the disk, a strange language, unknown to him, displaying some kind of information.

She turned the badge over and from a slot on the back, pulled out a flat disc the size of a half dollar, though slightly thicker. "I'll just leave this here," she said as she placed the disc high on a picture frame hanging in the hall where they stood. The disc attached itself. Breegan assumed it was a magnet.

"What is that?" he asked.

"It's a tracker. It will allow us to return to this exact place in space-time."

Breegan had no response. He pondered the fact that she seemed to genuinely believe in what she was telling him. He felt as though his worldview had turned into a drawing by Escher, where everything was what it seemed and yet was something else, too. A place where up could be down and left could be right at the same time. He felt oddly stable and yet as though he were falling through space at the same time.

She looked up at him, "Are you ready?"

"Ready for what?" he asked nervously.

"This," she said as she made one final stab at

the badge. A short, chirping musical tune emitted from the device, and the expanded geometric star began to rotate. As the star turned faster and faster, a chilling, howling blast of wind began to emanate from the badge. Sam grabbed Breegan's arm firmly as the lights of the room seemed to melt and meld and swirl around them.

"What's going on?" he shouted above the din. He looked around himself wildly, his eyes darting, trying to latch onto a solid surface. His clothing flapped in the breeze, his tie slapping him in the face.

"Relax! Try not to tense up," Sam said, her hair standing out almost straight behind her head. He didn't find this advice particularly helpful. By now the star was spinning so fast it was nothing but a dancing blur in her palm. "Here we go!" she shouted.

There was a flash of light, as bright as lightning, and a thunderclap that echoed through his bones. He felt a jolt, like an elevator stopping suddenly at the selected floor. Although the lights all around him were nothing but a swirling mass, he noticed a subtle shift in the color. The wind and the noise suddenly disappeared, as though sucked up in some enormous vacuum cleaner. His ears reeled from the violently abrupt quiet. His clothes settled down around him as the dust settled on the floor.

Breegan blinked a few times and looked around him. Everything had changed. The hotel hallway was gone. Breegan found himself in an alcove of another corridor, spotlessly clean, everything a sterile, shiny white. He saw no light fixtures; the light seemed to come from everywhere once. The floor curved gently into the walls, which, in turn, curved gently into the ceiling. The air was fresh and had nothing of the soft, stale odor of the hotel. Where the alcove met the hallway, a desk projected from the wall and behind it sat a person, apparently monitoring a computer built into the desk. Sam waved to the person and said something in a language Breegan didn't understand. The two held a brief conversation while Breegan listened, struggling to catch any phrase he might recognize. He didn't.

He noticed people moving up and down the hallway. People that looked like, well, people. *Would they be called "people" here?*, he wondered. They looked like nothing so much as ordinary humans from the planet Earth, but he began to realize that they were anything but. He had expected strange new life forms and was slightly disappointed that these transdimensional people seemed so similar. Even their clothing was not particularly unusual to him. Some of the fabrics he saw looked a little different, but in a way that he could not precisely put his finger on. They did have name tags, he guessed, printed in a language he could not understand, but other than that, he might actually be somewhere on Earth.

"Well, what do you think?" Sam asked, leading him out to the main hallway. She looked at him carefully, examining him for signs of a mental breakdown. She knew that sometimes the mental shock was too much for some of the visitors to this dimension, especially from the more primitive civilizations. It was an unfortunate side effect of bringing someone from another dimension to the station.

Breegan was looking around himself, shuffling slowly in a circle, trying to take it all in. He was at once nervous and as excited as a child in a candy shop. He was uncertain whether coming to this dimension actually gave him a better understanding of the day's events, or whether it just added to his sense of uncertainty. *In fact*, he thought, *even though I can't explain the transition from the hotel to this place, I really see nothing that would lead me to believe this is not, in fact, Earth.*

"Well," he said cautiously, "that was an impressive light show, but I don't know that I'm convinced of anything." In truth, his disbelief seem to be crashing down like an avalanche in his mind, but he didn't want to seem gullible. He wanted more proof.

"Fair enough," she said. "Follow me, then, and I'll see what I can do to convince you."

Sam started walking at a brisk pace as he trailed after. They made their way down the hall, turning at different intersections, and Breegan was soon disoriented. Incomprehensible signs appeared over doorways and at intersections, but they did nothing to help his understanding. Sam spoke briefly in passing to some of the people they met in the language he couldn't comprehend, but she introduced him to no one. Finally, they came to a set of double doors, which Sam pushed open with a familiar air, and they went inside.

It was an office space, apparently a police office. Even though the room was entirely new to Breegan, it had a familiar air, that familiar feeling of a busy police station. Sam continued to walk briskly, moving past the front desk, waving to various people and uttering brief words of greeting. Breegan realized that he did not understand the language they were speaking, though he could recognize the friendliness of the tone. She made her way into a small room with a desk, sitting behind it and propping her feet on the desk with a very practiced air. She gestured towards a seat and Breegan took it. Leaning back with one hand behind her head, Sam opened a drawer with the other hand and rummaged around.

"You'll need this," she said as she tossed a small object towards him. He caught it and turned it over in his hands, examining it. It was a badge identical to the one Sam had. He looked up at her, somewhat surprised.

"What's this?" he asked.

"It's a badge from the TDPD. Think of it as a visitor's badge. I wouldn't want you getting into trouble while you're here," she said, grinning. "We'll need to get it set up for you. Tap the center like this," she said, drumming out a short rhythm on her desktop. He hesitated, looking at her somewhat doubtfully, and then repeated the rhythm on the center his badge. The star snapped open, just as he had seen hers do only a few minutes earlier.

"Good. Now press your right index finger on the center of the badge and hold it there," she said as she tapped several buttons on a computer built into her desk and typed into its keyboard. A small panel in the wall behind Sam's desk snapped open and a bulbous stalk quickly emerged. As Breegan held his finger on the badge, shutters on the end of the bulb rotated open, like the lids of a mechanical eye, and green laser beams emitted from the pupil-like center, covering him in an electronic web of light. He started to move out of the beam, but Sam made a "sit still" gesture. He tried to relax, figuring at this point, he had trusted her with his life enough that he could trust her some more. The web of beams rotated over him, creating the outline of his body in 3D. After a few moments, the lids swung shut on the eye, cutting off the beams. Breegan let out his breath as the stalk vanished into it's hole in the wall.

"There," said Sam. "We've just made a biometric scan of you and loaded it into the badge. At some point, I'll have to teach you how to use it." She smiled at this. "One thing is very important, though. Never put the badge down somewhere without putting it into sleep mode. The computer polls all the badges every fifteen minutes and if it doesn't detect your life readings, it sets off an alarm. Lots of people will come looking for you."

"I'll try to remember that," said Breegan. "How do I do that?"

"When the badge is open, press your index finger to the disk and hold it there for a few seconds. It will flash a green light when you've held it there long enough. Then just remove your finger. It will close by itself and be in sleep mode. The next time you open it, it will go back into active mode."

"Ok," he said, I think I can remember that."

"Now give it a quick double tap," she said. He did so and the star snapped shut.

He examined the badge, turning it over in his hand. When it was closed, it just looked like an ordinary badge, perhaps a little thicker than most and with a geometric design not like any her had seen before. The badge was a tallish, narrow hexagon with the central star the dominating feature. No outstretched eagle wings, no soaring sky scraper, but it did have a familiar looking scroll across the bottom, emblazoned with an inscription he couldn't read. *"To Serve and Protect," I imagine*, he thought. At the top, engraved within a raised rectangle, were four glyphs… *"TDPD"?*…with the number 2134 just below. On the plain, flat back, there were four small dimples depressed around the edges of the surface and a half-moon shaped depression embracing a circle of material that looked like black glass in the center.

"Keep it on you at all times. We can use it to communicate with each other as well as teleport and perform a number of other tasks. It will take you a little while to get up to speed with it, but a good cop is never without his or her badge," she continued.

"Of course not," said Breegan, who looked the device over one more time and then shoved it into the left inside breast pocket of his coat. The heavy weight felt both strange and somehow comforting.

"Here, take this, too" said Sam. Breegan looked up just in time to see her toss a small object in his direction. He caught it and then looked at it, lying in the palm of his hand. It was a small device, not as big as a marble, of an irregular, oblong shape.

"Ok," he said. "What is it?"

"Just stick it in your ear," Sam replied. "It's a TranslatEar. That should help you out a little here." She was grinning at him, gesturing toward her own ear, as if Breegan might not understand what an ear was. He looked at her a little dubiously, shook his head, and put the translator in his right ear. He had to fiddle with it a little bit, but finally it fit snuggly.

"I don't hear anything," he said.

"Of course not, silly. I'm speaking English to you. I thought you would've recognized that." She winked at him, grinning broadly. She jumped out of her chair, headed toward the door, and said, "C'mon! Let's go see the prison."

Chapter Ten

S AM LED BREEGAN BRISKLY down the hall. Now as they passed people, he could understand them as they spoke to Sam. Breegan held his right ear and pondered what he was hearing. In one ear he heard the untranslated speech, the same gobbledygook he heard when they made their way to Sam's office initially. But in the other ear, the ear with the translator, he could hear the same person speaking in English, the same voice, the tone and inflection, but in everyday English. He shook his head and smiled...what will they think of next?

After a few turns in the hallway, they approached what was obviously a high security area. Thick steel...*would it be steel here*, he wondered, *or something else?*...doors with narrow slit windows blocked their path, An armed guard stood on either side of the doors, and another guard sat behind a computer console. Sam walked up to the desk and showed her badge to the guard. A green laser grid covered the badge and checked her number in the computer. The screen flashed a green, affirmative identification message and the guard turned to Breegan.

"And who is this?" he asked. Breegan was beginning to become accustomed to the dual-speech he was hearing, his brain naturally focusing on the English voice, the alien voice settling into the background as a sort of strange echo.

"New partner," Sam said. "Show him your badge, Breegan." He was a little nervous, but dug the badge out of his pocket and showed it to the guard. Again the green laser web danced across his badge and he, too, received the green flash of recognition from the computer. He was relieved by his clearance and shoved the badge back into his pocket.

"Destination?" asked the guard in a dry, official tone. Curt, to the point.

"Block 7a," said Sam. "The Joob."

The guard looked up at her, surprised. "They're still working on the investigation there."

"I know," said Sam, "I'm part of the team. Surely the computer told you that."

"Yes, of course," said the guard, though he really didn't remember whether or not the computer had told him that. Rather than risk the embarrassment of asking to rescan her badge, he decided it would be easiest to just take her word. In the end, Sam's confidence won the day and the guard waved them through the doors. As Sam and Breegan walked forward, the doors slid back into recessed pockets within the walls. As the pair passed, the doors closed quietly behind them.

As they made their way down the hallway, the intersections they passed were marked with signs that Breegan couldn't read.

"Too bad the translator doesn't help with signs," he said. He had been somewhat overwhelmed by this new dimension and was feeling decidedly old-fashioned. This apparent oversight in alien technology made him feel slightly better, a little less in over his head.

"Hmm? Oh, yes," said Sam. "I should've shown you. Open your badge." She dug her badge out and tapped the center in the rhythmic pattern she showed him earlier, just in case he didn't remember. He secretly appreciated the reminder as he got his badge out and did the same.

"Now read the sign through the disk," she said, holding hers up to eye-level, demonstrating.

He did so and noticed that the central disk, which he had assumed was an opaque, black glass, actually functioned as a screen. Holding the badge between the sign and his eye as though he were looking through a camera lens, he could see the sign on the disk, but instead of the alien language, he could now read the sign in English. His feeling of, not superiority, but perhaps less inferiority, began to deflate. He performed the quick double tap to close his badge and returned it to his pocket.

"This way," he said glumly, jerking his thumb down the hall in the direction that he now knew led to Block 7a. Sam didn't seem to notice his frustration and they walked on. Unlike most office buildings on Earth, the halls were arranged at odd angles, seemingly at random, almost never a simple right angle. Some intersections had more than four directions one could travel in, sometimes five or six halls came together and sometimes a corridor would move away from the junction at an incline, either up or down. Breegan wondered how the geometry of the building fit together. At first he had to pull out his badge at every intersection to read the signs but he quickly learned the correlation between the strange symbols on the signs and the translation he read on the badge's screen. Before long, he could recognize the symbols he was following and no longer needed to use the badge.

After what seemed to Breegan like an eternity of walking, they finally reached a heavy double door that Breegan could see was labeled, "Block 7a." Through the windows in the doors, he could see a lobby-like area with a large bank of windows on one wall and a few desks. Next to the door was a small, blue square on the wall. Sam reached out and touched this button with one hand while holding her badge up to the familiar green laser grid that emitted from the wall above the blue button. A computer voice said, "Access granted." The doors clicked and then opened, sliding into the walls. Sam walked through and Breegan followed.

An officer was sitting at one of the desks in the room and turned toward them as they entered. He seemed to recognize Sam, gave her a curt nod, and then turned back to the report in his hands. Though the architecture of this jail was still foreign to Breegan, the room had a familiar feel, a place where cops spent a lot of time waiting, watching, filling out paperwork, and drinking coffee. Sam walked to the wall of windows and gestured for Breegan to follow. As he did, could hardly believe what he saw through the glass. A sweeping vista so vast, his mind could not understand how it fit into the building. A lush, tropical jungle sprawled out in front of him, fading into the distance, not constrained by any walls that he could see. The foliage, a multi-hued green mass, stretched up toward the orange sky, the branches and leaves swaying in a fresh breeze. There were clearings that he could see and in those open spaces he could see clusters of Joob, huge, fierce-looking, and intimidating even when seen from this safe vantage point.

"This is the rest of Janx's tribe," said Sam. "Their cell covers about 1,000 acres in your Earth terminology. All the plant life is real, though the ecosystem is artificial, of course," she said, as though such a remark was totally unnecessary. To Breegan's mind, though, it wasn't so obvious. Peering through the glass, it was as though he were looking at the world outside, a hotel room's view of a tropical jungle. The view didn't lead Breegan to believe he was looking at an artificial construct, a free-range prison.

"The plant life act as a filtering system for the

air and the water is filtered. Weather is artificially generated as well as seasons. It's all carefully controlled to simulate life on the Joob home world," she continued. "The Joob have a central village you can see over there," she gestured and Breegan saw, for the first time, a gathering of huts in the distance, scattered randomly around one of the clearings in the jungle.

"How many of them are there?" asked Breegan. "How can you keep track of them in such a large space?"

"There are 373 Joob in this cell currently. The number fluctuates occasionally with births and natural deaths. They're all tagged with a biochip, inserted subcutaneously," said Sam. She move to one of the desks that had an array of large computer monitors. Sam deftly touched several buttons on the console and a list began scrolling down one of the screens. "We can see a listing of all the Joob and their current location at any time, and on this display," she touched a few more buttons, "we can see them on the map." On the screen she indicated he could see a satellite view of the jungle with tiny red dots moving, infrared images of the Joob. She manipulated the console again and demonstrated how the system could zoom in on any location within the cell.

"If they're all chipped, why can't we just track Janx's chip?" Breegan asked.

"That would be nice, wouldn't it?" she replied, the sarcasm heavy in her voice. "We, of course, tried that, but it didn't work. We don't know what happened to the chip...either it's malfunctioning or he's managed to remove it somehow. In any event, it's not working. I told you, he's hyper-intelligent. There's a reason he's the leader of the tribe." She smiled wryly and shrugged.

"I see," said Breegan. He gazed out the window, the incredible vista spreading out before him, his mind still trying to take all this in. "How large is this building? Are there many cells like this one?"

"Size?" said Sam. She chuckled and shot Breegan a look like a mother watching a child learning new things. "Dimension isn't really a fixed quantity, as you suppose it is on Earth. It can be," she paused, searching for the right word, "adjusted. Stretched, compacted, altered as we need. The same technology that allows us to teleport through time and dimensions makes it possible to make a huge cell like this fit within a given space. To be honest, I don't understand the details, I just know it works. That's how I manage to have sprawling flat while only paying rent for a one bedroom." She smiled again with that contented look of someone whose world was completely settled, completely normal.

Breegan stared at her for a moment, trying to decide if she was pulling his leg or not. After a moment, he decided he wasn't sure but that it didn't really matter. He perceived the cell as being huge and, functionally, it was. Whatever the cell's actual physical dimensions might be was irrelevant. It would still take a long time to walk across the cell on foot.

"So what happened," he asked. "This cell seems secure, how did Janx get out?" He said this, not as an accusation, but merely as a curious remark. After all his years on the force, he knew that sometimes things just happened. Despite your best precautions, sometimes things went wrong.

"Well, that's the curious part," said Sam. "We're not really sure. As you can imagine, there are any number of precautions, any number of layers to the security in this building, but somehow he managed to create a portal and get to your dimensions. The boffins haven't quite figured it out yet." Her face hardened a little, her professional dignity ruffled a little, and she squinted out the window, as if the answer was lying somewhere in front of her and she might find it if she could just focus on the right spot.

"We use drones to run errands within the cells. Sometimes just close up surveillance, sometimes administering medicine, sometimes delivering pack-ages. People are never allowed in the cell to perform those sorts of tasks." She gestured toward the other officer in the room and Breegan could see that his monitor showed the view from one such drone, sweeping low over the jungle canopy, following one of the Joob as it walked down a trail.

"In the span of a week, we had a number of drones go missing," she continued. "There are the occasional mishaps with the drones. Mechanical failure, autopilot error, wind sheer accidents, etc. There are larger drones that we can send in to retrieve wreckage, but this week was different. A total of four drones were lost, two regular drones and two rescue drones. Janx apparently managed to ambush them and from their parts he created a portal repeater….a mirror of sorts that allowed him to piggyback on the main transportation portal… the one we just came through…in another area of the building to make his escape. Ingenious of him, actually, but it was a one way ticket. The device he built couldn't actually go through its own portal, it couldn't generate its own portal because it was reliant on the feeder portal in this building. So he was able to get out, but now he's stuck in your dimension." She shrugged and looked at Breegan with the clean look of the confessed, one who has nothing to hide. He appreciated her candor and felt as though at least some of the pieces of this puzzle were beginning to fit together.

"Have you seen enough," she asked, "or do you need further convincing?"

"One more thing," said Breegan. "How did you get to Earth? Why did you come through the basement if your badge let's you teleport when and where you wish?"

"It's not that simple," she said. "Traveling through time and space isn't an exact science."

"What do you mean?"

"It's not like you can track someone who teleports. There are no breadcrumbs through space-time. So we had no idea when or where he went. But he left behind his portal repeater with his destination settings intact. I had to come through his portal in order to find out where he went. Simple, really." Breegan was surprised that this explanation made sense to him. He was coming to terms with this new reality.

"Why can't you just travel back to the moment right before Janx came through the portal with a squad or two of police and catch him there?" Breegan asked.

"The portal is not very precise. The time-space stream moves by at an incredible rate. Picking the exact place to step out of the current can be tricky. Imagine being on a moving sidewalk traveling hundreds of miles per hour and trying to step off at one specific inch along the path. Easier said than done without some sort of reference point. Also, you have to worry about the butterflies."

"The butterflies?" he said. Just when things seem to be making sense, he thought.

"Yes, the Butterfly Effect. You're familiar with this?" she asked.

"Perhaps you could refresh my memory," he said.

"It's a theory of cause and effect. If a butterfly flaps its wings over the Amazon, does it cause a tornado in Texas? That sort of thing." She said this as if that would make everything clear. Breegan thought that she was either being deliberately cryptic or that she was giving him credit for being more intelligent than he actually was.

"Um, yeah. That's not really helping me," he said.

"Space-time is actually a very delicate balance. Even supposing we could come to the exact moment before he appeared, if I came with a large force of men, the introduction of such a large extra-dimensional mass could tip the balance there. It might cause his portal to open somewhere else entirely or somewhen else. That's one of the reasons why the Transdimensional Council limits the number of travelers to two."

"One of the reasons? What are the other reasons?" Breegan asked.

"The costs involved, of course. It's very expensive to operate the transportation portal. Have to stick to a budget, you know." She was smiling again.

"Of course," he said. Apparently bureaucracies are the same no matter where or when they are, he thought.

"Ok," he said, shaking his head and giving a dry grin. "I've seen enough. Let's get back."

Chapter Eleven

"SHE'S A TRANSDIMENSIONAL COP?" asked Steve, although his tone indicated less of a sincere question and more of a sincere question of Breegan's sanity. "Chasing a demon across space-time?" They were sitting in their makeshift operations center in the maintenance office of the hotel where Janx made his first appearance.

"Well, yes. I agree, it sounds a little...far-fetched. It's not the sort of thing you hear of every day, I'll admit," said Breegan. He felt a little ridiculous explaining something that he felt in his heart to be true, but which he really didn't rationally believe in his mind. But explain he did, and the explanation came out better than Breegan was expecting. If you didn't let the irrationality interfere, his explanation made a lot of sense. Steve seemed to sense this, too, and was eventually swayed, if not to fully accept what Breegan was telling him, then to at least not totally reject the idea. It was a start.

"In a way," said Steve, "it makes more sense than anything else we've come up with so far." Though a highly rational person, Steve didn't mind substituting irrationality, especially when rationality wasn't doing its job. You have a badge, after all," he grinned at Sam. Injecting his own irrationality into the conversation made Steve feel a little better. "I've never heard of this particular police force, but a badge is a badge." His face reflected a combination of relief and disbelief. It looked as though the scale could still tip either way.

"So what are your thoughts about these missing cell phone parts?" asked Breegan, turning to Sam and hoping that Steve was persuaded enough to go along for now.

"Gentlemen," she began, after taking a deep breath, "I believe Janx may be trying to assemble his own key to the portal." She paused to let the implications of this settle in.

"His own key?" asked Steve. "I don't get it. Why would he want to get back into the…uh…transdimensional prison?"

"I don't think he wants back in, Steve," said

Breegan. "If I am following Sam's logic, I believe he intends to get the rest of his tribe out."

"Precisely," said Sam. "And, gentlemen, I believe that it's clear what will happen in this dimension if a couple hundred Joob are allowed to roam free here." She looked at them significantly, but there was no real need. Both men fully understood the implications of such an event.

"Are they armored?" asked Breegan. "I mean, if you shoot one, can you kill it?"

"Yes, certainly," said Sam, "if you have the proper weapon. Your Earth devices with their simple projectiles won't be very effective. The Jube are somewhat armored, as you say. They have tough skin and bony plates in vital areas. The bones in their head, for example, are so thick they can use it as a battering ram. They also have extraordinary physiology and heal at an incredible rate. Also, they are extremely intelligent. They won't let themselves be easily found in the open. Against an unarmed human....well, we've seen what happens in that instance." The entire group nodded in general agreement. There was a pause while each gloomily considered his or her own thoughts on the subject.

"But, is it really that easy?" asked Steve. "Just throw together a handful of phone parts? You'd think someone would've made it more difficult that that."

"Well, yes, you would. And in many dimensions, it would very nearly be impossible. Not many dimensions have technology in such abundance as you do here," said Sam. "Many dimensions are uninhabited or inhabited only by single-celled organisms. Had he ended up in one of those dimensions, it would've been worse, actually, than staying in the transdimensional jail. I don't think you realize how privileged you are in this dimension, from a grand perspective."

"Privileged or not, we've got a problem on our hands. Janx can get as many cell phone parts as he needs. Most people at this convention will have at least one cell phone, if not more. Not to mention tablets and laptops…" Breegan's voice trailed off.

"Surely it requires more than just cell phone parts," said Steve. "Please tell me there's some fancy, top-secret part that he won't be able to find."

"Well, fortunately, it's not just a matter of parts for a key. In order for the key to work, there must be a certain conjunction of planetary forces, which admittedly happens more than one might expect," Sam chuckled. Apparently, transdimensional travel was amusing to her. In fact, many things seemed to amuse her. "But one also has to be in the right inter-dimensional location, a bridge location, as it were. A place where the two dimensions in question are close enough to affect a bridging action. And lastly, there is an enormous energy requirement. It was really just an amazing stroke of luck for Janx that the bridging location was in conjunction with the electrical power mains of this building. That's what caused the breakers to trip here...the portal consumed so much electricity that it overloaded the circuit. Not, of course, before the portal opened and he could come across."

"What about this conjunction of planetary forces?" asked Steve. "What does that mean?"

"I think you people refer to it as a planetary alignment," said Sam.

"You mean the planets have to be lined up perfectly?" asked Breegan. "That doesn't happen very often, does it? "

"It doesn't necessarily mean that the planets are in a straight line. Their forces can be aligned through particular resonant angles. Just as the seem-ingly small and distant mass of your Moon can cause the bulk of all the water on Earth to shift on one axis of the planet, these alignments of planets can have dramatic effects here. That's what caused the earthquake you experienced this morning. And that force exerted enough influence on that fabric of space-time to make the bridge possible."

"So he'll not only have to assemble a key, he'll have to be in the right place at the right time to be able to use it," said Steve.

"Precisely!" said Sam. "Very good, Steve!"

"So when and where will that be?" asked Breegan.

"Well, I think we know the where but I'm not certain on the when." I will need access to some fairly sophisticated computing technology. Do you think you can arrange that for me, Breegan?" she asked.

"I'm sure we can," said Breegan. "Just what kind of computers are you talking about?

"Oh, I'm sure the local public library will have what I need," she said.

Breegan looked at her blankly. He blinked.

"I don't have a card," she explained. "You'll have to get me in."

Breegan continued to stare at her. Finally, he began to speak. "In the meantime," said Breegan, deciding to ignore the preposterousness of this exchange, "we need to develop a plan to try to catch this guy. We can't just wait for the next time he can open the portal. It's clear that he feeds on a pretty regular schedule. We can almost set our watches by his feeding plan."

"Yes, and he stays away from the main areas of congestion," said Sam. "But I think he'll stick close to the convention. He's not stupid. He knows he can blend in very easily here and feed at will."

"And gather his phone parts virtually at will, too," said Steve. "It really is a pretty ideal situation for him."

"So what we need," said Breegan, "is more security in the out of the way areas of these hotels."

"I think that's about all we can do here at this point," said Sam. "But I need to do some research to determine the next time he can create an interdimensional bridge."

"I wish we had a picture that we could distribute to our security people," said Breegan. "Steve, you check the surveillance cameras to see if you can spot him near the murders. I'll call the Chief of Police and get more men down here. And then, Sam," he paused, drawing in a deep breath and still not believing what he was about to say, "I'll take you to the library."

Chapter Twelve

I T WAS A SHORT drive across downtown Atlanta to the main branch of the public library, a modern art pile of blocks shaped like an upside down pyramid, threatening to topple and crush those hapless passers-by who might be in the way when the fateful moment arrived. Climbing the stairs to enter the glass doors gave one the impression of being fed into the mangle of an old-fashioned washing machine, though on a much larger scale. But the knowledge they needed was inside, so into the jaws they went.

At the front desk, Breegan flashed his badge and explained that they needed to use a computer. Behind the counter, a young clerk stopped poking her cell phone and looked up, somewhat annoyed. "Do you have a library cards, *Sir?*" she asked, slightly emphasizing the last word. She wore huge hoop earrings and an expression of boredom of similar size. Apparently the wad of gum she was chewing was also of impressive proportions, because she was unable to chew it with her mouth closed.

"No, as a matter of fact, I don't," Breegan replied, somewhat sheepishly. "Look, this is important police business."

"Don't the police have any computers of their own," she asked, thoroughly unimpressed by the badge.

"Yes, of course, they do, but I don't have time to drive across town to get back to my office. This is a matter of life and death!" said Breegan, his voice growing louder as the sentence went on. Pulling out the "life or death" card made him cringe inwardly, feeling like a cheap Hollywood detective. But it really was a life or death situation, so he reassured himself that it was ok.

"I can't help you unless you have a library card, *Sir*," again the emphasis. "If you would like to fill out this paperwork, we can begin the process to get you one. Do you have a utility bill with you or something else to prove your identity?" She held out a clipboard with the necessary forms attached.

Breegan smacked the clipboard away and roared, "Listen to me you officious, smug…"

"Is there something I can help with here?" asked a middle-aged woman wearing a tweed jacket over a thin turtleneck sweater. She had appeared unnoticed. Behind her, two security guards were spreading out to approach Breegan from either side. Her name tag declared her to be the Supervising Librarian - Adult Department.

"I hope so," Breegan said, still glaring at the clerk, who only rolled her eyes and resumed poking at her phone. "My name is Detective Breegan, APD, and this my colleague, Detective Spade," he gestured to Sam. "We have important police business and need to use a computer."

"Certainly, Detective. Do you have a library card?" she asked.

Breegan took a deep breath, his face turning red. He closed his eyes and counted to ten, just like his therapist advised him to do in such situations. "Look, Missus…" he said, reading her name tag in further detail.

"Ms.!" she interrupted.

"Excuse me, Ms. Marion," he continued, "I do not have a library card. But, surely and exception can be made in this case. This really is vital police business." He looked at her hopefully. She didn't appear to even be considering his plea.

"Perhaps if Detective Breegan starts filling out the paperwork," said Sam, gesturing to the stack of paperwork now scattered on the floor, enough paperwork, it seemed, to mortgage a house, "I could use a computer? In anticipation of his expected receipt of said card?" She smiled sweetly, gently nodding her head as she did so. Breegan began picking up the papers and mashing them into an acceptable heap for the clipboard.

"Well," said Miss Marion. "That is slightly unusual." She paused to consider the possible ramifications as Sam continued to gently nod at her. Her imagination was unable to generate an image of future bibliographic anarchy stemming from this slight deviation in library procedure, so she said, "I suppose we can slightly rearrange the sequence of events. Just in this one instance," she said somewhat doubtfully, a sudden image flashing in her mind of a long line of police officials at the desk, demanding materials without the necessary card.

Miss Marion made a gesture of dismissal to the security guards and said, "If you'll come with me." She led them past the circulation desk and toward the central computer area of the library. They didn't stop there, though, as Breegan expected, but moved down a small side hallway that held private meeting rooms. She stopped at the first empty room and drew a key out of her pocket.

"Since this is official police business, I thought you might rather have a little privacy for your work," said Ms. Marion as she slid the key into the lock and opened the room for Sam. She reached in and turned on the light, and then said, "Please, Detective Spade, make yourself at home." She held the door open as Sam moved into the room. "Detective Breegan, if you would come with me."

Sam quickly settled into the room, turning on computers, and rummaging through her pockets. Breegan followed Ms. Marion out of the hallway, back past the main computing center, and toward the executive suite. She ushered him into her office and asked him to be seated. "If you would please fill out these forms, I will expedite your card." She smiled icily. Breegan sat back in the chair, sighed, and started scribbling on page one. By the time he reached page three of the application, he grimaced as writer's cramp set in.

"I will check on your friend," said Ms. Marion, as he shuffled sheets of paper to reach page four. He grinned at her as he continued to scribble furiously, though the grin was less a friendly grin as much as the grin of someone who was imaging how nice it would be to commit bodily harm to someone. The only sound in the room was the scratch of pen on paper and the muttering under his breath.

He was finishing up the fifth and final page of the application when Ms. Marion burst back into the room.

"Detective! We have a serious problem on our hands. Please come with me!" Her face was flushed with livid rage, and her formerly neat hair bun was showing signs of distress, too. He followed her down the hall toward the computing center, noting that her pace was considerably quicker than it had been the first time he made that trip. She practically skidded around the corner toward the room where she had left Sam. They reached the room and she rushed in.

"Detective Spade, what is the meaning of this?" said Ms. Marion, her voice brimming with near-hysteria.

Sam looked up from the computer screen, a picture of nonchalance, and said, "I'm sorry, is there a problem?" Breegan looked into the room and immediately saw Ms. Marion's concern. There were four computers in the room, all with their covers removed and a spiderweb of wires criss-crossing the room, connecting them together. On the screen in front of Sam, lines of data scrolled up the screen at an impossibly fast rate. Impossible, that is, for her to actually be able to read the data whizzing by.

Ms. Marion stammered. She stamped her foot and tried to speak, but her pique overcame her power of speech, at least momentarily. Finally she was able to utter, "What is the meaning?…What are you?…Do you have any idea?" she sputtered. She gestured madly about the room and stamped her foot again for emphasis, in the off chance that her displeasure was not readily evident. Breegan rubbed his neck with one hand while the other instinctively groped for his pack of cigarettes.

"Hmm?" said Sam. "Oh, this?" she jiggled some of the wires running around the room. "This machine doesn't have quite the computing power I require, but I have been able to patch into the processing cores of these other machines and have achieved a satisfactory improvement. It was quite necessary, I assure you."

If Ms. Marion's level of indignation was falling, this comment sent it through the roof again and she once again lost what little ability to speak that she had so recently regained. "Detective Breegan!" she spluttered.

"I just need five more minutes," said Sam, looking at him. "This modification is completely reversible. Just let me finish these calculations, and I'll have these machine back to their previous, dullard status quick as Bob's your uncle! Give me a pen, Breegan." He did and she smiled sweetly at Ms. Marion, turned back to the computer screen, and began to scribble furiously on a piece of paper. Breegan could see that the paper was a page ripped from a phone book containing a map of Atlanta, and he surmised that Sam had "obtained" the page from the library.

Spittle appeared at the corners of Ms. Marion's mouth and her face was an unhealthy shade of red. She was still unable to speak, but her eyes darted back and forth between Breegan and Sam and her bun was becoming more unraveled by the moment. Breegan took her gently by the elbow and led her from the room.

"The police department will, of course, pay for any damages, Ms. Marion," Breegan said in a gentle voice. "There's nothing to worry about." He walked her back to her office and found a bottle of water in the refrigerator in the corner. He opened it for Ms. Marion and held it to her lips, giving her a little water and letting only a little dribble down her chin. He did not dare attempt to dry off her neck. She seemed to be no longer aware of her surroundings, simply staring at the wall and ignoring his inquiries as to her status.

Breegan decided it was time to collect Sam and make a departure from the library. He took one more look at Ms. Marion, still staring but now beginning to make quiet, gibbering noises. He started to leave the office, but turned back to gather up the paper work for his library card application. He pulled the forms off the clipboard with a snap and stuffed them into his pocket. As he left, he quietly turned off the lights and pulled the door shut behind him.

By the time he reached the room where Sam had been working, she had returned the computers to their former state. There was no sign of the elaborate web of wires that had been there just moments before. He glanced around and thought about asking what had happened to her impromptu network, but then thought better of it.

"C'mon," he said instead. "We've got to get out of here."

Chapter Thirteen

BREEGAN AND SAM PULLED up to the hotel and parked in the drop-off loop. Breegan waved his badge at the valet who came out to protest, and they left the vehicle in the no parking zone and entered the hotel lobby.

"The job does have some perks," he quipped with a grin. His comment was largely lost on Sam, who was concentrating on the notes she had jotted down at the library. She was mumbling to herself, and he had to grab her elbow several times and guide her around other people on their way into the lobby and across the floor. Breegan led them to the coffee shop just off the lobby. He bought three strong, black coffees—no fru-fru mocha-frappa-latte drinks for Breegan. Steve had, out of necessity, become accustomed to Breegan's coffee drinking preferences. Sam had never tasted coffee before and so had no inherent complaints. Carrying the coffee in a cup holder, they headed to the maintenance office that had become their base of operations at the hotel.

She opened the door to the office for Breegan, since his hands were full of coffee, and then followed him inside. Steve was waiting, grinning widely, and looking for all the world like a kid sitting before the Christmas tree. He gratefully accepted the coffee proffered by Breegan and took a sip.

"Wow! That's strong!" he said. "Still out of cream and sugar, are they?" Though he was used to Breegan's coffee preferences, he still took every opportunity to needle him about it. "You know, it's odd that every coffee shop you go into is out of cream and sugar, Breegan."

"Do you want the coffee or not?" asked Breegan, who, after all the time they had worked together, still got a little riled over Steve's coffee remarks. Steve chuckled and let the subject drop.

Sam was cautiously sipping the, to her, mysterious, black liquid. It was scalding hot and so warranted caution, but also the sharp, bitter taste was new to her.

"This is a curious choice of beverage," she said,

trying to decide whether or not she liked it. She took another sip, made a face, and decided that it needed further evaluation.

"So?" said Steve. "Are you going to ask me? Don't you want to know what I found?" He was obviously bursting to give his news, but he enjoyed the give and take of the slow reveal. In another life, he might have been a stripper.

"Ok," said Breegan, familiar as he was with Steve's methods, "what have you found?" Breegan could gauge Steve's excitement and realized that Steve must have some excellent news to be as delighted as he clearly was.

"I thought you'd never ask!" said Steve. "Look at this." He swiveled in his chair to face the computer screen. He made some quick movements with the mouse and a screenshot from a security camera appeared on the screen. The mostly-in-focus shot showed the demon, a massively muscled creature with a jagged horn emerging from his forehead. Janx was walking away from the camera, but had turned his torso back toward the lens and appeared to be glaring at the camera. The shot was not very detailed, but did give a good idea of just how enormous the demon was.

"He was probably aware of the camera," said

Sam. "As I said, he is incredibly intelligent and hyper-aware of his surroundings. It's not going to be easy to catch him. I really am somewhat surprised that you managed to get him on a camera at all, at all." She spoke at a rapid pace and an unusual, wide-eyed look was on her face. She took a long swig of coffee. "This really is the most remarkable drink. We don't have anything like this where I come from!"

Breegan and Steve considered her for a long moment and then Breegan said, "C'mon, Steve. This isn't all you've found, is it?" Steve needed coaxing, enjoyed it, actually.

"No, as a matter of fact," Steve said, with a grin, "it's not." He clicked away at the mouse and soon another security shot appeared, this one form a little further away. It, too, wasn't the most detailed picture you could wish for, but in it, the demon was walking near two humans and so, gave a good indication of his height.

"This is great, Steve," said Breegan. "We need to get these out to our people and hotel security. This will really help." He was smiling and feeling as though they were finally making some progress in the case.

Steve, however, just looked at him like the cat

who just swallowed a canary and slowly shook his head. There was a wicked gleam in his eye.

"What?" said Breegan, incredulously. "Is there more?" He couldn't believe there could be more, but it was obvious from Steve's demeanor that there was.

"This is child's play," he said, smugly. "Look at this!" and he swiveled in his chair again. Again he played with the mouse and another photo appeared on the screen. Breegan involuntarily flinched. This time the picture was startlingly detailed. Janx couldn't have been more than a few feet away from the camera when the photo was taken and every horrible feature of his face was clear and distinct. The jagged horn, the folds of skin that would direct blood into his mouth, even the palpable feeling of hatred in his pupilless, yellow eyes was apparent.

"Holy…" said Breegan. "Where did you get that?" he asked, unable to take his eyes from the screen.

"You'll never guess!" said Steve, enjoying the impression he was making on Breegan.

"I know I won't," said Breegan. "Just tell me, please." Sometimes humoring Steve took too long.

"I had a hunch, so I checked the remaining cell

phone parts and found a memory card, from the woman in the bathroom. I plugged it in and, sure enough, she had snapped a picture of the demon just before she was killed." He smiled triumphantly. It certainly was a coup. The three pictures Steve found would help tremendously with spotting the killer.

"Great job, Steve!" Breegan said, slapping him on the shoulder. "Make sure these get out to all the security teams. And let's hope this gives us an edge."

"She was taking pictures in the bathroom?" asked Sam. "What in the name of the Seven Portals was she doing using her camera in the bathroom? Is this some strange Earth tradition? I don't know of anyone who takes pictures in the bathroom. Is there any more of this wonderful beverage? Could we get some more? I would really like some more of this!" Her sentences ran together and the look in her eyes was nearly manic.

"I think maybe that's enough coffee for now," said Breegan, shaking his head. *Sam's dimension must be truly miserable if it has no coffee.*

As he considered this, the phone in his pocket began to ring. He dug it out and stabbed at the screen. He thrust it to his ear and said, "Breegan.

What is it? Why are you telling me about this? I'm in the middle of a murder investigation. Uh huh. Yes, we're on it." He stabbed the phone again and thrust it back into his pocket. "C'mon, let's go. You're not going to believe this."

Chapter Fourteen

THE LATEST MESSAGE FROM dispatch told them they needed to move down the street to one of the other hotels hosting the convention. Fortunately for them, one of the maintenance men, whose office they had commandeered as the base of operations for their investigation, had shown them that there was a side entrance to the maintenance area of the hotel, so they could come and go without having to traverse the surging mass of humanity in the lobby. Once on the street, though, they still had to move with the circus parade of costumed people flowing back and forth between hotels and nearby restaurants.

Breegan and Steve walked in silence, grim looks on their faces. Their recent discovery of photographs of the suspect had cheered them up temporarily, but after the initial excitement wore off, recent events reminded them that their progress was still much too slow. As they struggled to find the clues they needed to stop the demon, people were dying. Any mistake they made was paid for with the life of some innocent. On top of that, the demon was a killing machine and he planned to bring more of his kind to this dimension. How many people would die then? How long before the human race would be decimated? These thoughts weighed heavily on the detectives and bolstered their determination to succeed. Still, determination did not guarantee success, and they knew that they had their work cut out for them.

Sam, on the other hand, was still deep in the grips of her caffeine-induced mania. She babbled non-stop as they walked down the street, commenting on everything from the costumes she saw to the decorations in shop windows to the clouds in the sky. She was fascinated by everything and apparently could not filter her remarks. More than once her vocal critique a of costume garnered an angry look from the subject in question, and Breegan had to mumble apologies, grab her by the arm, and drag her along the sidewalk so she would have less time to speak.

The area of Atlanta where the convention flourished was a hilly section of the city. Traveling from one hotel to another in the array of hotels that composed the compound of the 'con, attendees generally found themselves on a steep incline, up or down depending upon which particular hotel served as the destination. Precious little of the trip was likely to consist of a flat, horizontal slide across the street, and Breegan, Sam, and Steve were not that lucky on this particular walk. They found themselves headed up a hill, like salmon against the stream of the incredibly crowded sidewalk, pressing forward, sidestepping, always struggling.

Two blocks up the street they came to the hotel they needed. They were met at the door by another uniformed policewoman, Breegan and Steve flashed their badges, Sam was explained, and the officer led them across the lobby. This hotel had the same highly polished, cookie-cutter architecture as the main hotel of the convention, designed to awe the guest with the sense of enormous space and opulence. Besides some difference in the precise shape of the enormous space and a variation of the bland beige and off-white color scheme, they could've been in any of a number of hotels in downtown Atlanta. The slow progress they made through the crowd allowed Breegan to consider all this in detail.

Instead of heading down some out-of-the-way hallway, they continued to slowly make progress through the throng to a large side hall that was clearly involved in the proceedings of the convention. Uniformed police officers were taping off an area that, if the signs were to be believed, was being used for a blood drive. It was a large, lobby-like area at the center of a cluster of convention rooms, the area mostly taken up with neat rows of chairs covered in a throng of convention-goers. Velvet ropes marked queues to different meeting rooms and people were either busy standing in a line, waiting to get into one of the meeting rooms, or sitting in chairs, waiting to enter another meeting area. On the left side of the room there was a large seating area for people waiting to give blood.

"Seems like an odd place for a blood drive," muttered Breegan, to no one in particular.

"Not really," said Steve. "Believe it or not, the people who come to these kind of conventions are very civic-minded. As I understand it, the blood bank does a killing…" He shot the others a nervous glance, realizing that his comment was somewhat inappropriate. He cleared his throat and continued, "But you say the blood drive has been robbed? How do you rob a blood drive?"

As they approached the scene, badges were flashed, credentials established, and the trio gained access behind the shiny, yellow tape slung like a giant spiderweb across the area. The uniformed police struggled to keep inquisitive convention goers at a distance, not any easy task in the crowded and confined space.

As Breegan entered the area, he could see that a great disruption had taken place. Many folding chairs and camp tables had been knocked over and the room was a complete mess. Medical supplies were scattered across the floor, mingled with disposable cups and the cookies and chips handed out to donors after they gave blood. Although the room could obviously hold a couple dozen people giving blood, the only people actually in the room were the blood drive workers. They were all wearing identical T-shirts, huddled in one corner of the room, talking nervously, and waiting to answer questions for a police officer.

One of the officers on the scene introduced

Breegan to one of the workers from the blood drive, apparently the person in charge. She was an older lady, with curly silver hair and an abundance of skin hanging from her neck and wiggling under her forearms as she nervously pulled at her fingers. There was a band-aid on her forehead and her glasses looked slightly bent. Her face was pale, and there was a wild look in her eye. Breegan could tell she had seen something startling.

"Hi, I'm Detective Breegan," he said, shaking her hand, "and these are my associates," gesturing with his other hand toward Sam and Steve. "So, tell me what's going on here," said Breegan. As he let go of her hand, he slipped his hand into his coat pocket and pulled out his notepad and pen. He stood with pad and pen in hand, head cocked to one side, doing his best to appear attentive.

"I'm not sure where to begin, it all happened so quickly and violently. I've never had anyone rob a blood drive before. I mean, who would do such a thing? So many donations…how will we ever…"

"Okay, why don't we try to relax a little and calm down. Would you like a cup of coffee or something?" asked Breegan. She nodded her head and placed one hand on her chest while steadying herself against the table with the other. "Steve, let's see if we can find her a cup of coffee please." Steve nodded and quickly moved off in search of coffee. Breegan gently took the woman's elbow and led her to a chair. He settled into the chair next to her and placed his notepad and pencil on the table beside them. She took several deep breaths, and he could see that she was beginning to calm down a little.

"Why don't we start over?" He said, smiling. "Let's start with your name, please."

"Oh! I guess I forgot all about that. Where are my manners?" She chuckled and a little more natural color came back to her face. "My name is Sally Minot. I'm the director of the blood bank." Her words came at a more reasonable pace now.

"Do you have a blood drive at the convention every year?" he asked.

"Oh yes, the blood drive of the convention is always a big success. We get an amazing amount of donations here." She began the sentence with a broad smile, but it quickly began to fade. "Of course, this year will not be so successful."

"And why is that?" asked Breegan.

"Well, a man just came in here and took a large part of the blood donations from today. I just don't understand why someone would do that." Breegan could see tears beginning to well up in her eyes and her hands began to tremble slightly. Steve returned just then with a steaming cup of coffee, which he handed to Sally. She cupped it with both hands, gently blowing on it and sipping it cautiously. Breegan was grateful for the slight pause, hoping that she would remain calm enough to answer his questions.

"What can you tell me about the man?" asked Breegan, his pen poised over his notepad.

"He was wearing some kind of costume," she said. "Some kind of large, black monster. He looked sort of like an evil unicorn. He had one horn in the middle of his forehead. If he was supposed to be from a movie, I've never seen it. Some of these people come up with the strangest costumes." She started to shake her head but then winced and gently placed one hand on her forehead, where the band-aid was.

"Are you ok?" Sam asked, resting a hand on Sally's shoulder.

"I'll be fine, sweetie," she said, adjusting her glasses and taking another sip of coffee. She patted Sam's hand and smiled at her.

"What else can you tell us? How tall was he?"

"He was huge! He must've been about 6 1/2 feet tall, I guess. He had to stoop and turn sideways a little coming through that doorway. He could've been a football player under that costume. And he was very strong. He knocked people out of his way like he was shooing flies."

"What exactly did he take?" asked Breegan.

"He took a lot of the blood we collected over the last few hours. After drawing the blood, the bags are stored in coolers until we can transport them back to the blood bank. He took two of the coolers, one in each hand, and drug them out of here. Each cooler holds forty pint bags, so that's eighty donations gone."

Breegan looked at Sam and said, "That's a lot of blood."

"A lot of blood, indeed," said Sam. "That much blood would go a long way."

"It would have gone a long way," agreed Sally, although she did not understand what Sam and Breegan meant. "We could've served a lot of patients with that blood."

"Yes, I'm sure you could have," said Breegan. "Did you see which way he went?"

"No, I didn't," said Sally, her hand gently touching the bandage on her forehead again. "He knocked me down and it took me a minute to find my glasses. When I did find them, he was out of sight."

"I see," said Breegan, his head down, scribbling on to his notepad. "I think that's all we need from you right now, Sally. We may be in touch later, though. Thank you for all your help."

As he stood to go, he shook her hand again and stuffed his notepad and pencil into his pocket. He gestured for Sam and Steve to follow him to an empty corner of the room so their conversation wouldn't be overheard. They huddled around each other, speaking quietly.

"80 pints of blood!" said Steve. "How long will that last him?"

"A good while," said Sam. "That's about eight feedings for him." They looked at each other, the implications dawning on them. "The good news is, there shouldn't be any more murders. At least, that is, until he brings the rest of the tribe here."

"Yes, but the bad news is, with this supply of blood he can go to ground, hide out. This will make it much harder to find him," said Breegan, shaking his head. "We need to find out where he went," said Sam. "Surely someone saw him. A huge monster dragging a couple of coolers down the hall would be a memorable sight, wouldn't it?" There was a hopeful tone in her voice, edged with uncertainty. Given the nature of the 'con, unusual sights were a dime a dozen. People would surely have noticed the demon, but the novelty of it would last only a few seconds before some other "unforgettable" sight came along to bump the image of a cooler-toting demon out, replaced by an endless cycle of the extraordinary.

"Let's split up," said Breegan. "Steve, you start canvassing the immediate area and I'll move down the hall. As quickly as people are coming and going, I'm not sure what we'll find, but it's our best chance." Steve nodded and walked over toward the group of other blood drive workers to see what they could tell him.

"I need to head back to the maintenance office to go over my data," said Sam. "If you need anything, call me through your badge." With that, she turned and headed down the hall toward the hotel entrance.

Breegan had nearly forgotten the heavy new badge Sam had given him, nestled in the left inside pocket of his coat. His hand patted the unfamiliar lump, as if to reassure himself that it truly existed. As he watched her threading her way through the crowd and disappearing from view, he thought over the events of the day and wondered if things could get any stranger. He shook his head, as if that would dispel his troubled thoughts, and then headed into the hall himself.

Chapter Fifteen

BREEGAN LOOKED RIGHT AND left as he walked away from the blood bank and into the hallway. *How do you find a demon in a room full of demons?* he wondered. He moved to a vantage point that allowed him to see the entire lobby area, as well as the halls leading into it. He stopped and leaned against the wall to contemplate his next move.

He watched the constant flow of people in and out of the room. The sounds and smells of people coming in and out of the area provided an ever-changing, but somehow constant, counterpoint to the visual parade. Occasional loud laughter or shouts, fleeting glimpses of pungent scents or particularly strong perfume, served to highlight the otherwise monotonous murmur of the crowd, the nondescript scent of a large body of people moving in close proximity to one another. He realized that there were probably very few people left in the area that had been there when the robbery occurred. How could he find someone who could give him any clues?

As he stood there ruminating, he noticed that not all the people were moving in and out of the area, as he had initially assumed. Over to one side of the lobby was a member of the hotel staff, a janitor with a broom and a dustbin with a long handle, sweeping up random debris and checking to see if the garbage cans needed emptying. Breegan realized that this man had probably been working in this part of the hotel all morning and might be a good lead. He moved toward him, digging his badge out of his pocket as he crossed the room, dodging a group of teenage girls in cartoon costumes.

"Good afternoon," he said, flashing his badge. "I'm Detective Breegan with the APD. I'd like to ask you a few questions." The man paused in his work, leaned on his broom, and looked at Breegan, eying his badge somewhat skeptically. Breegan wondered how many times a costumed cop had approached this man during the course of the 'con. He put his badge away and drew out his notepad.

"Sure," said the janitor, apparently convinced that Breegan was an actual detective and not just a costumed convention-goer. "What can I help you with?" He spoke around the toothpick jutting out from the corner of his mouth.

"Were you working in this part of the hotel when the excitement happened over at the blood drive?" he asked, gesturing over his shoulder toward the taped off space.

"Yes, I was, though it didn't seem like much out of the ordinary. These 'con people are always shouting and yelling and jumping all over the place. Bunch of hooligans, if you ask me," he said. He shook his head, pulled handkerchief out of his back pocket, and blew his nose loudly.

"Did you see a person dressed as a giant, black demon carrying a couple of coolers away from the blood drive?" ask Breegan, nodding his head and secretly agreeing with the man.

"Carry, my ass! He was dragging them, and no wheels on them coolers. Just look what he did to the carpet!" He pointed to tracks in the carpet. "Must've been pretty heavy to do that. The hotel manager's gonna be pissed." Breegan followed the drag marks across the carpet. At one point where the coolers crossed a seam, the carpet was torn a little.

"Thanks" said Breegan. "I appreciate your help." He snapped shut his notepad and moved quickly to examine the marks in the carpet, thrusting the pad into his pocket as he went. The marks moved toward one of the side halls, away from the main area of the convention and toward the guest rooms. Breegan followed and stopped short at the edge of the lobby, where the carpeting gave way to tile.

"Damn," he swore gently. "What now?" He peered at the tile floor, wondering if his luck had run out. But as he moved his head from side to side, something caught his eye, just a little way down the hall. He moved toward it, moving left and right, and changing his height, trying to find a good angle to see whatever it was. He pulled out his cell phone and fiddled with it, turning on the flashlight. He bent down a little and held the phone low, shining the light towards the thing he thought he saw on the floor. The low-angle light caused the object to come clearly into view. It was a scuff mark on the waxed tile floor. The mark was faint, but Breegan scanned across the hall near it, looking for more. He saw another mark, parallel to the first, and just the right distance away…the width of a large cooler.

Now that he had an idea how he could track the demon on the tile floor, he felt relief. His luck was still holding on. He stood and looked around the room, searching for Steve. It took a few seconds before he spotted him, and, by some strange stroke of luck, when he did, Steve happened to be looking right at him. Breegan waved his hands and gestured for Steve to come to him. Steve began to move in his direction, so Breegan returned his attention to the hallway floor.

"What's up, boss?" asked Steve.

"I think I'm on to him," said Breegan. "Help me follow these tracks." Breegan pointed out the marks in the tile to Steve and when they both had an idea of what they were looking for, they moved down the hall, looking like crazed drunks, bobbing and weaving, rushing forward, then coming to a stop, waving their phones back and forth like a couple of Keystone Kops, with cell phones instead of giant magnifying glasses The scuff marks were not consistent, but there were enough of them to be able to follow. Fortunately there weren't many people in that hallway to disturb the marks or to witness their bizarre, weaving progress.

"I just hope he doesn't get on an elevator," Breegan muttered as he made his way in slow pursuit.

"That would be a problem, wouldn't it," said Steve.

They came to a junction in the hallway where the marks were even fainter than the rest. In the dim light, the marks appeared to go down two hallways at once.

"I guess we better split up," said Steve.

"I'm not sure that's such good idea," said Breegan, "but I'm also not sure we have much of a choice." He rubbed his chin with one hand while contemplating the hallway. Unable to decide which marks were the right marks to follow, he finally made up his mind.

"I guess you're right," said Breegan. "You go down that hall and I'll take this one. If you see anything at all, call me."

"Sure thing," said Steve, and he began moving down is assigned all, bobbing and weaving as he went.

Breegan shuffled down his hall, trying to move as quickly as he could while still deciphering the faint scratchings. Several yards down the corridor he came across a side table up against the wall. The marks he had been following ended at the feet of the table, a perfect match.

"Damn," he swore again. He turned on his heels and moved swiftly back in the direction he had just come. He turned at the intersection where he and Steve split up and hurried after him. He couldn't see Steve in the hallway ahead and realized that the demon must've turned down a side hall. Soon he came to a corridor intersection and saw the tracks indeed turned. He still couldn't see Steve.

When the trail finally led to a hall full of guest rooms, the floor reverted to carpet and the signs were clear again. Breegan picked up his pace, his heart beginning to race a little. He began to consider the fact that he was in pursuit of a creature who possessed incredible physical strength.

He came to a junction in the hallway where a few openings converged. There was a short hallway that led to a door with a sign that read, "Hotel Staff Only." On the other side of the main hall, a side hall with a sign that read, "Pool & Workout Room." Guest room doors stretched out in front of him and behind, a symmetrical demonstration of the laws of perspective. The tracks in the carpet led into an alcove with a sign that read, "Vending/Ice." Breegan followed but stopped short just after he entered the recessed space. There, in the corner of the room, were the two coolers. He stood up straight and put his hands on his hips. *Why would the demon drag the coolers all this way and then abandon them?* he wondered. *And where is Steve?*

He took one step forward into the small space and stopped, his blood suddenly running ice cold. From the corner of his eye he saw a shape and he knew instinctively what it was—who it was. He turned and saw Steve sitting on the floor, his head tilted to one side, his phone clutched in his right hand, the fingers on his left hand twitching slightly. Breegan rushed toward him, saw the gaping hole in his chest, and knew that there was no hope. Breegan knelt beside Steve and touched his arm.

"Steve, I..." Breegan said. He didn't know what to say. Telling Steve that everything would be all right seemed ridiculous. It was very clear that everything would not be all right. Still, he wished he could say something to ease Steve's passing. He closed his mouth in a grim smile, squeezed Steve's arm, and looked into his eyes. As he did, he could see the glimmer of life starting to go out in Steve's eyes, his eyelids beginning to droop.

Steve's lips quivered gently, soundlessly, as if he

were trying to say something. Breegan leaned closer, putting his ear near Steve's mouth.

"What is it, Steve?" he asked. Glancing down, he could see Steve's lips moving, but he heard nothing.

"It's ok, Buddy, rest easy. It's ok," Breegan said, sitting back on his heels and patting down his pockets for his pack of cigarettes. He gazed at Steve's face, waiting for the end. Suddenly Steve's eyes snapped open, staring hard at Breegan, his lips moving again, trying to speak, trying to warn.

Breegan heard a deep, rumbling exhalation behind him. The hair stood up on his neck, and he broke out into a cold sweat. He jumped up and started to spin around, his right hand grabbing for the snub-nosed revolver in his pocket. As he turned, the huge, black form of the demon filled his sight, a blur of motion. He whipped the revolver out of his holster and snapped off a shot. He heard the wet smack of bullet tearing into flesh and the demon's earsplitting roar. Then his world went black.

Chapter Sixteen

S AM MADE HER WAY back through the halls and across the lobby of the hotel, pausing to get a cup of coffee from a small shop. *Thank the Seven Portals Breegan gave me some money,* she thought. She sipped at the hot beverage as she walked out of the crowded hotel and onto the teeming sidewalk. *As first impressions of a planet go, this one is rather pleasant, if one doesn't count the murders,* she thought. *Everyone dressed up in festive costumes and having a good time, and the coffee, of course, makes everything better. I really must find out why we don't have coffee back home. Perhaps I should introduce the Joob to coffee. Maybe they would be a little less cranky. I have to think about that.*

She walked down the sidewalk, headed toward the hotel with the maintenance office where the day's events began. It was hot and muggy, the air clinging to her a little like water in a pool. It almost felt like wading through the air rather than just walking through it. The humidity had a way of amplifying smells, too. Savory scents coming from restaurants, the choking chemical stench coming from the exhaust of vehicles driving by, the pungent, acrid odors coming from alleys and darkened doorways she passed, which apparently had been used as restrooms.

Sam was eager to determine Janx's next steps. She had little doubt that he would complete his portal key. She knew he was too intelligent, and there were too many resources here, for him not to succeed. So it really was a matter of anticipating his plan and coming up with a way to thwart it. Especially since he seemed to be too wily to track down and capture amongst all these costume demons.

She reached the main hotel and entered through the maintenance door, bypassing the crowded lobby and halls. She moved more quickly now that she was out of the throng, and, since the maintenance office was just a short distance from the side entrance, she was soon settling into a desk chair. She set her cup of coffee down and reached into a pocket of her coat. She pulled out the scraps of paper she had obtained at the library and spread them out in front of her on the desk. Opening the desk drawer, she rummaged around, looking for a writing instrument. She found a stubby pencil amongst the strange conglomeration of debris inside the drawer— paper clips, bottle caps, assorted rubber bands, an adjustable wrench, and a handful of mangled ketchup packets. She eyed the chewed-on pencil dubiously but could find no other writing utensil. She shrugged, closed the drawer, and focused on the papers in front of her.

The complexities of transdimensional space travel are really too complicated to go into here, but suffice it to say the mathematics involved are not readily calculated without access to a supercomputer. The machines Sam cobbled together at the public library could hardly be called a supercomputer. It would be generous to call them an "okcomputer." But it had done the bulk of the heavy lifting on the calculations, Sam only needed to complete a few matrices to finish the computation. She looked in the other drawers in the desk but could find no paper. She slid her chair sideways to be able to reach a printer sitting on another small desk and took some paper from its tray. She wheeled back to her desk and began to draw the necessary tables.

Sweat began to bead on her brow as she realized that perhaps she should've paid more attention during Mr. Holliwizgig's class. Of course, when you're a teenager sitting in transdimensional algebra class your mind is usually somewhere else, anywhere rather than there. *One never thinks that one day one might actually have to do that type of math on one's own. I mean, what are computers for, anyway?* She paused to examine her work, chewing on the end of the pencil. *Do you carry that one or do you invert it?* She leaned back in her chair and stared up at the ceiling, trying to remember. She had assumed this pose in Mr. Holliwizgig's class, obviously too often. *Carry or invert, carry or invert?*

Her mind drifted back to those long, tortuous mid-afternoon classes with Mr. Holliwizgig. Nestled directly in the middle of the indolent, sweaty afternoon block of classes, transdimensional algebra was a combination of a physical trial to stay awake and a mental challenge to understand even a portion of what the teacher was saying. Lunch was far enough behind her that her full stomach was doing its best to drag her down into sleep, while the dismissal bell was far enough ahead of her to seem like an impossibility. So there she sat, suffering in silence along with the rest of her classmates, daydreaming of going outside, running free from the mind-numbing world of transdimensional algebra, free from understanding or even caring whether to carry or invert.

Just then word "invert" lit up in Sam's head like a flash of lightning. Sometimes the solution to a problem is sitting right in front of you, so obvious and plain to see that it becomes invisible.

"Of course!" she said. "We can easily invert the beam! Why didn't I think of this sooner?" She leapt from her chair and pulled her badge out of her pocket, forgetting about her math calculations.

"I must tell Breegan!" she said, her face covered in a wide grin. She performed the rhythmic tap to open the badge and then swirled her finger on the central glass disk. The disk briefly flashed a confirmation that it was attempting to call Breegan. She leaned against the edge of the desk and crossed her ankles, feet stretched out, holding the badge in front of her, waiting impatiently for Breegan to pick up. The badge rang five times and then chirped out a tone that told Sam there was no answer on the other end. She bit her lip and frowned at the device.

"Why doesn't he answer?" she asked no one in particular. Annoyed, she called him again, moments ticking by, but still no reply. She tapped the disk again and said, "Give me Breegan's status."

"No status available," said the badge, after a short pause. "No life readings detected." Sam realized that Breegan must have put the badge down somewhere without putting it into sleep mode. He knew better than to do that. Sam's heart began to beat a little faster as annoyance turned into concern.

"Show me Breegan's location!" she said, snatching up her papers and thrusting them into a coat pocket. She ran for the door.

Chapter Seventeen

BREEGAN WAS AT THE bottom of a well. The well was dark and cold, the weight of the water pinning him in place, unable to move. He shivered involuntarily as even colder currents swept over him through the frigid water of the well. His body felt almost frozen. Beams of light stabbed down through the murky water, barely illuminating the darkness. But the well was peaceful, and he had no fear, no concept of drowning entered into his mind. Strangely, he could breathe, and for a moment he thought about that, wondering about the impossibility of the situation.

Something caused him to stir—a sound, a smell, perhaps something touched him. Like a hand reaching down into a well and pulling him up, something was dragging him back from the blackness. And just like a bucket being drawn from deep in a well, he gradually approached the light with a rushing sound in his ears and a gradual subsiding of the weight upon his body. As he became more conscious, his senses seemed to return to him one by one. The deafening sound in his ears grew louder and louder until, after a few moments, the roaring subsided and was replaced by the sound of his heartbeat and his ragged breath. At the same time, the darkness of the well slowly became a dim light, growing brighter and expanding in his view, as if the sun were peaking down into the shaft of the well, growing stronger, bathing him in light until the brightness was almost blinding. Even though his eyes were closed, he squinted, and the light began to fade a little. Then he noticed the smells. He could smell himself, the sweat of the day, his stale aftershave. There was another sweaty smell, too, one that he didn't recognize, strong and musky. He noticed the faintly musty smell of the space around him, and he tried to connect it to a location.

The smell jarred loose a memory. He remembered getting up that day. He remembered taking a shower, getting dressed, his first cup of coffee. He remembered going to work and getting the call to head to the convention for a murder investigation.

This last memory caused a chain reaction in his mind, and the events of the day flooded back to him. He remembered following the tracks of the demon from the blood bank, remembered stumbling upon the two missing coolers, and he remembered Steve's pierced body, his quivering fingers, and his dying attempt to warn Breegan. He recognized the sound that came from behind him—the sound that he heard just before everything went black, the sound that he heard in the room with him now.

His eyes snapped open. As the light hit his eyes, so too did a stabbing pain. The comfort of his unconsciousness was stripped away like warm sheets being yanked off in the middle of winter. Suddenly, he was quite aware of the throbbing pain coming from the back of his skull and the sharp, cutting sensation at his wrists and ankles, clearly from being tied to the chair on which he was sitting. He looked around the room and tried to get his bearings. It was a typical hotel room, two beds, a large dresser with a TV on top, a desk, a few chairs...nothing out of the ordinary. On the table was a pile of the cell phone parts Janx had been collecting, along with the contents of Breegan's pockets, including his revolver. The covers on one of the beds was in disarray and the sheet torn. Stacked in one corner of the room were the two coolers from the blood drive, and, on the floor next to the coolers, Breegan could see a small pile of empty blood bags. He vaguely wondered what the housekeeper would think of that. Surely Janx had put the "do not disturb" sign on the door.

Then he remembered the sound that had been playing over and over in his mind. The deep, rumbling sound of breathing that could only come from a enormous pair of lungs. And he realized that he could hear that sound now, that it had been the almost gentle background music of the movie his life had become. He turned his head, trying to see his assailant, and his neck instantly protested the movement.

"So," said Janx, with a voice so deep and vibrant that James Earl Jones himself would've been jealous. "You are finally awake." Breegan could hear slow, heavy steps approaching and he thought for a moment that he could feel the floor tremble with each step. He wondered if he should brace himself for the end of his life, which suddenly seemed short and pointless. Surely not. Janx would not have bothered to render Breegan unconscious and bring him to this hotel room if murder was his only motive. Breegan gulped involuntarily and braced himself for something worse than death.

He tried to remain calm in this first face-to-face encounter with the demon. The surveillance video pictures, shocking though they were, hardly prepared him for the real-life meeting. Janx was impressive. His height and bulk spoke of incredible strength, even when Janx was merely standing in front of Breegan. Seeing the jagged, hollow feeding horn on Janx's forehead in person made the murders seem understandable — they became logical, entirely rational, and inevitable. From this distance, he could see that traces of fresh blood were on the horn, trickling down toward the horrible, fanged mouth. Steve's blood, he thought. He clenched his jaw tightly, the heat of his anger rising throughout his body. Breegan fought to keep thoughts of his own close encounter with the feeding horn out of his mind.

"What is it you want?" asked Breegan. "Why have you brought me here?" Behind his back he flexed his arms, trying to loosen his bonds, but they were tied quite securely. His efforts only managed to send new waves of pain through his wrists.

"Struggle all you like," said Janx. "I have complete confidence in my bindings. And besides, your efforts amuse me." Breegan was surprised to see a smile spreading on Janx's face. It hadn't occurred to him that such a murderous beast could find happiness in something.

Janx drug one of the empty chairs in front of Breegan, and, turning it around so the back of the chair faced Breegan, the monster sat down, casually, like it was entirely normal to hold a tête-à-tête with a bound figure. Janx crossed his arms on top of the back of the chair and rested his chin on top of them, the act highlighting even further his size and strength. Breegan gritted his teeth, stifling another involuntary gulp. His eyes were drawn to a pockmark the size of a bullet wound in Janx's left bicep. Dried blood highlighted the ragged hole, but the flesh was closed, healing at an incredible rate, as though he was shot a couple of weeks ago, not an hour or so ago. Janx followed Breegan's eyes to the wound and laughed.

"Your puny weapon can't harm me. Amusing, really. Puny weapons for a puny species." Janx wiped his hand across the scar, brushing some of the blood away. Breegan realized with a jolt that the mark looked even less like a wound now than it did when he first noticed it just seconds before. Sam was right, human weapons would be of little use against Janx and his tribe.

"I have come here from a long distance," Janx said. "I'm not sure if your species can comprehend, exactly, the concepts involved, but the important thing is for you to understand that I am not from here." Breegan snorted at the obviousness of this statement and it occurred to him that Janx didn't know that Breegan had seen the transdimensional prison and knew quite a bit more about Janx than Janx knew. Breegan knew that little bit of information was his only advantage over Janx. He decided to keep this to himself and let the demon rant a little.

"You have seen the results of my feeding, and you surely know that I must continue to find blood in order to survive," Janx continued. "Also, you have seen that I am adequately equipped to sustain myself in this environment." As he spoke, he casually lifted one finger up to the horn, wiped up a trace of blood, and then licked the blood off the finger, relishing the taste.

"I must compliment your species," said Janx. "You have a most delightful flavor!" He laughed a deep, dark, rumbling chuckle that reverberated in Breegan's bones. Breegan jerked against his restraints, glaring at Janx, wanting nothing more that to get his hands around the demon's throat, even though, rationally, he presented no more physical threat to Janx than a kitten would to Breegan.

"You fucking pig!" shouted Breegan, feeling powerless but wanting to lash out at his captor. Of all the cases he'd been on over the years, it suddenly occurred to him that this was the only one that really mattered. Individual murders might affect a large group of people…family, friends, coworkers… but this particular murderer had the ability to impact his entire species.

Janx had been licking his finger, but now his hand shot out, the back of his hand connected squarely with Breegan's jaw. The impact was incredible. Breegan's head snapped to one side and blood sprayed from his mouth. His vision dimmed, and he nearly lost consciousness again. His head drooped, blood and spittle dribbling down the front of his jacket.

"I beg your pardon," said Janx, "What was that you said?" He had the politeness of an English butler and Breegan found himself dimly wondering where Janx had learned his English. Perhaps, like Sam, he had watched some movies from the 1950s.

"You won't get away with this," Breegan whispered, the feeble sound being all he could muster.

"Oh, on the contrary," smiled Janx. "I will get away with this. Because I have the skills, the strength, and the cunning I need. And I have the anger. You see, when I was wrongfully imprisoned, it wasn't just myself that suffered. It was my entire tribe. The Transdimensional Justice Department felt that I and my people had become a threat to their way of life, and that it was best if we were all locked away. So they took a very minor offense and exaggerated the scope and detail and used that as an excuse to incarcerate me and my tribe, when all we really wanted to do was just enjoy an existence of freedom, unfettered by their contemptible morality." Janx's anger was palpable. He stood up, still straddling the chair, the tendons on the back of his hands in sharp relief as he gripped the chair back firmly. His pupilless yellow eyes almost glowed in their fury and his brow, deeply furrowed in anger, made Janx's face even more terrible to behold.

"I will have my revenge!" said Janx. The level of his voice had barely risen, but the force behind his words made it seem like he was shouting. The demon stood still for a moment, a statue dedicated to the possibility of revenge, and his look changed from one of anger to that of enjoyment, savoring the joys of the vengeance that he knew would be his. The tension seemed to flow out of Janx, and he sat back down.

"I tell you this because I want you to understand that the suffering your species will soon endure is not of my making. This is the doing of the Transdimensional Council and the cowardly race they represent. Also, there is nothing you can do to stop me, to stop us." Janx chuckled again and reached out to Breegan's face again, this time gently tracing the curve of his face with a fingertip, gazing at Breegan with the gentleness of the butcher before he slaughters the lamb. Breegan jerked his face away.

"What do you mean us?" Breegan asked.

"I'm sorry," said Janx, back in his butler mode. "Did you think that I would enjoy all of this sweet human blood by myself?" He smiled at Breegan again, his lips parting slightly to reveal Janx's fangs and the impression of a benevolent, happy being faded. "In a very short time, I will be joined here by the rest of my tribe. I know the Transdimensional Police think they have created the most ingenious prison, the most escape proof prison possible, but as we can see by my presence here, they were wrong."

He smiled again, an even larger smile, the pitying one Breegan's classroom teacher gave him when he gave a silly answer to a question.

"That doesn't really answer my question," said Breegan. He wondered if he was pushing his luck with Janx, but knew that he might be able to take advantage of the demon's hubris and get him to reveal details of his plans. *Although*, he smiled ironically to himself, *there's no reason to believe that I'll ever get out of this room alive.*

"No, it doesn't, does it?" Janx laughed again. He seemed to enjoy toying with his prey. "In a very short time, as I said, I will open another portal into the cell I formerly occupied at the transdimensional prison and I will bring my entire tribe here. As you have seen, we will have no trouble feeding here. We will fade into your cities and towns and woodlands, and we will become a new nightmare in your collective psyche. We will become the newest bogeyman you use to frighten your children into behaving. Except we will be real — we will snatch up those who walk alone, we will seize children out of their beds at night, we will cause people to simply vanish. And there will be no holy water, no silver bullets to vanquish us."

"You don't have the technology to do that," said

Breegan, his anger rising again. Janx rose from his chair and stepped over to the desk where all the cell phone parts, along with the contents of Breegan's pockets, were lying.

"In point of actual fact, you are correct. I don't have the technology…yet," he said. "As you can see, though, I am getting close to having it." He held up a device, a conglomeration of cell phone parts connected together at odd angles and appearing nothing like a cell phone. Then he started to dig through Breegan's things, gently dragging a finger through the pile, like someone stirring a bowl of soup as it cools. His hand paused over the pile.

"And it's entirely possible that you have just provided me with the final piece I need," he said, picking up Breegan's' transdimensional badge and holding it up. Breegan could see an indicator light blinking on the badge, but couldn't remember what it was supposed to mean. Janx turned the badge, examining it. He performed the rhythmic tap on the central disk of the badge and it snapped open. Breegan wondered how Janx knew how to operate the badge, but decided it was just one more thing he didn't fully understand.

"Yes," Janx said with his fang-filled grin, "this will definitely provide the last piece I need." He stroked the badge with an eerie affection, seeming to forget for a moment that Breegan was in the room. In his mind, Janx was enjoying the upcoming reunion with his tribe. Breegan was slightly surprised at the depth of emotion he could see on Janx's face.

"But I still need to deal with you," said Janx, abruptly coming back to the present. He laid the badge down gently on the table and turned to face Breegan squarely. Janx raised himself to his full height and his already imposing chest seemed to swell even larger. He reached down and grabbed Breegan's chair, lifting both the chair and Breegan effortlessly until their eyes met at the same level.

"I *am* feeling a bit peckish," said Janx.

Chapter Eighteen

"THE BLOOD I STOLE from your blood drive is satisfying, but there really is nothing like warm, fresh blood," continued Janx. He licked his lips and smiled, as he began to lift Breegan even higher.

"I hope you choke," said Breegan through clenched teeth. He struggled against his restraints but still could not budge them. *So this is the end*, he thought, feeling strangely detached from the event.

The door burst open in a shower of sparks, an acrid cloud of smoke billowing through the doorway. Sam dashed into the room, one hand waving the smoke from in front of her face, the other holding a small weapon. But as fast as she moved, Janx moved even faster. In one swift motion, he tossed Breegan aside, snatched up his patched together device and Breegan's badge from the desk-top, and threw himself through the room's window. The sound of glass shattering mixed with that of the report of a weapon as Sam managed to get off another shot at him. Janx moved too quickly, though, and she only hit the window frame, the shot exploding in a smoky ball of sparks, just as the door had.

Breegan and his chair had bounced on the nearest bed and then fell to the floor, wedged precariously between the two beds that filled the room. Seeing that he was still alive, Sam quickly scanned the room for other threats and rushed to the window, peering down into the alley below.

"Damn," she said. "No sign of him." She turned her attention to Breegan, who lay moaning and grunting on the floor. Despite fresh blood on his face from the fall, he was still trying, unsuccess-fully, to free himself from his bonds.

"I could use a little help here," he said. He had a little difficulty talking with his face pressed against the carpet.

"A little *more* help, I should say," said Sam, relieved that she had arrived in time and feeling a little more than pleased with herself. "I should also think you might say, 'Thank you,' too," she said with a smile. She holstered her weapon under her left arm and knelt down to untie him.

"Thank you," he said, with feeling. The realization of what almost happened was reaching his rational brain, which had, until just now, decided it wasn't going to pay any attention to actual events. He shuddered, considering what might have happened had she not arrived, and let relief wash over him. "Thank you," he said again.

Sam couldn't untie the bindings holding Breegan to the chair; the knots were pulled too tight. Janx had tied Breegan with strips torn from a sheet from one of the beds. She reached into a pocket and pulled out a small knife and began sawing at the cloth. The sharp knife quickly cut through the material, freeing Breegan's limbs. As the blood flowed back into his hands and feet, so, too, did a fiery pain. Sam had some difficulty extricating him from the chair and the gap between the two beds. First she lifted the chair off him and set it down next to the bed. Then she helped him struggle to his feet. Finally, she helped him sit on the edge of the bed, and checked him over for injuries.

"That's some gun you've got there," he said.

"What, this?" she said, pulling the weapon out from its holster. She held the gun out in the palm of her hand. Breegan took it from her and examined it. It looked similar to the snub-nosed .38 that he carried, but where Breegan's gun had a revolving cylinder to hold the cartridges, Sam's had a bulbous cylinder with cables snaking across the surface. There was no hammer and the grip engulfed his hand as he tentatively sighted down the barrel. As he did so, a laser aiming point appeared on the wall, though he hadn't noticed any laser sight.

"It's just a standard issue plasma gun. All the detectives carry one," she said, accepting the gun back from him and returning it to its holster.

"It packs a pretty good punch," he said, eying the door, which smoldered, shattered on its hinges. The window frame, too, fumed; the smoke was being gently pulled out the broken window on an invisible current.

"It has a couple of different settings, depending on what you're shooting at," she said. "Saves you from having to carry more than one weapon."

"Well, it seems more useful than my .38," said Breegan. "I managed to shoot Janx when he attacked me and Steve..." his voice trailed off, the memories of Steve's final moments flooding back in to his brain.

"Steve is dead," he said. "Janx killed him. The

usual way." He sat rigidly, his fists clenched in tight, white-knuckled balls in his lap. He trembled slightly, partly in rage and partly, he was surprised to realize, in sadness. It had been so long since he had felt strong emotions. He thought the job had drained him of the ability to feel much at all, but Steve had been the only person left in Breegan's life to whom he felt close, even though they were only work colleagues. Sam laid a comforting hand on his shoulder.

"I'm so sorry," she said. "He was a good friend?"

"The last one I had." He grinned ruefully and shook his head. "It's funny how you can be surrounded by millions of people in this huge city, but only be close to one." He stared into the middle distance, like staring into a bottomless pit, wondering why things happen the way they do. But he realized that when you go looking for trouble, sometimes you find it. Steve was more of a lab tech than a field guy, but he was a cop. *He knew that the job was dangerous and he accepted those risks, just like the rest of us*, Breegan thought. He jerked his focus back to the here and now, his jaw clenched, determination mixing with the rage boiling through his veins.

Breegan stood up tentatively, not quite trusting

his legs yet. He stepped gingerly toward the table and began reclaiming his things, including his snub-nosed revolver, which apparently held no interests for Janx. He marveled at the number of items he normally carried with him. With everything in the proper place within his vast array of pockets, he didn't really notice how many things there were, but when he saw them all piled up together in one spot, he couldn't help but notice. He started to reload his pockets mindlessly, an automated routine he performed every morning.

"I managed to shoot him, just before he clobbered me, but the wound was nearly healed by the time I woke up here."

"Yes, I told you your weapons wouldn't be very effective against him. My plasma weapon not only punches holes in things, it also disrupts neural patterns. It would disrupt his ability to heal, at least for a while. But even with the right gun, it will be hard to take him down," she said.

Breegan was in a slightly shocked condition, rubbing his wrists, and still trying to come to grips with the fact that he was not impaled. He looked down at the last item to go back into his pockets, a small, battered flask. He unscrewed the top and took a long pull, wincing a little as the amber liquid washed over a cut on his lip. He offered the flask to Sam. She took it, gave it a sniff, and then took a sip.

"Mmmm. That's pretty good," she said, and took another sip. "Thanks," she said. She handed the flask back to Breegan and sat down heavily on the bed. "Well, that was exciting, wasn't it?"

"Yes," said Breegan. "I don't think I could take much more excitement like that." He gave her a feeble grin.

"I think I've figured out what Janx is up to," said Sam. "If he can manage to complete his portal key, we may have a problem on our hands."

"He took my badge, my new badge, that is," Breegan said, somewhat embarrassed. "He said it will be the final part he needs to complete his key."

"He did?" she said, jumping up from the bed. "It may help him complete his portal, but he doesn't realize we can track him with it!" She yanked her badge out of a pocket and quickly had it open.

"Show me Breegan's location," she said to the badge. On the screen, a small red dot appeared on a map, moving quickly away from them.

Chapter Nineteen

S AM AND BREEGAN DASHED through the doorway and down the hallway, passing a couple of surprised looking hotel guests who had come into the hall after hearing the explosion of the door being blasted open. Sam waved her badge in their direction as they ran by, yelling, "Official police business!" The pair of guests hugged the hallway wall to let Sam and Breegan pass, their overcoats billowing in the self-made wind of their rapid pace.

Sam continued to hold the badge in front of her as they ran, using the map as a guide. They swiftly reached the end of the guest room hall and burst into the lobby area, their footsteps switching from muffled carpet to clattering tile.

"We have to go down," said Sam, breathless.

They paused and looked around the lobby for some way down to the floors below…an elevator, a stairwell, something.

"That way," said Breegan, pointing toward a stairwell door on the other side of the lobby. They started to run again, this upper-level lobby thankfully uncrowded. Sam led the way, slamming open the stairwell door with her shoulder. They flew down the stairs, their footsteps hammering out a syncopated beat. They spiraled down and around until they came out on the ground floor of the building. Pushing open the bottom stairwell door, they rushed out into the crowded main lobby of the hotel, their progress instantly ground to a near halt.

"C'mon!" shouted Breegan, taking the lead. "We don't have time to wait." He pulled out his badge in one hand and his gun in the other and started shoving his way through the crowd, yelling as loudly as he could, "Get out of the way! Police business! Make a hole!" Sam followed suit, and their combined commotion seemed to have a positive effect. The crowd started to part, apparently thinking this was another impromptu performance of a couple of costumed 'con attendees. Some people applauded, and some even snapped pictures of Breegan and Sam as they rushed across the lobby. More than one turned to a friend and asked what movie that was supposed to be. They crossed the wide space faster than they thought possible and burst out into the fading sunlight.

"Turn right," said Sam, and they headed down the sidewalk toward the main cluster of hotels hosting the 'con. "Hurry, he's moving fast." They rushed past the alley where Janx had leaped from the hotel room window and through the crowd on the sidewalk, Breegan continuing to yell and wave his arms like a madman. The performance was as effective on the street as it had been in the lobby and the crowds continued to part and let them through, mostly unimpeded.

As they crossed a street against the light, a car screeched to a halt just inches from Breegan's legs. He fell across the hood of the car, arms splayed to stop his fall. He pushed himself back upright and waved his badge at the angry driver within. The driver waved an appendage back at him. Breegan slapped the hood of the car and continued running after Sam.

"This way," she said, turning left across the main boulevard and toward the entrance of another hotel. They rushed up the granite stairs, past steel statues of angry, alien-looking lions and a group of 'con goers who were resting on the steps, relaxing and watching the spectacle of DemonCon. The air conditioning washed over them as they entered the lobby, feeling colder than usual on their sweaty skin. Sam felt delicious chills running down her back. This lower-level lobby was tiny and almost immediately turned into a combination stair-case and escalator up into the main part of the hotel. Up they ran, taking two steps at a time where they could, but the crowd slowed their progress.

"We're catching up," said Sam, her breathing ragged but her eyes gleaming. The stairs emptied onto a large, packed mezzanine. There were two rivers of people jammed into the area, one shuffling into the building, one shuffling out. Breegan's shouting act was no longer working, but he continued to shove his way through the crowd, Sam staying close in his wake.

"Go to the left, toward that hall," she said, reaching up to point over his shoulder. He nodded and continued to plow his way through the throng. As they reached the opening of the side hall, Sam said, "Be careful, we're getting close."

Breegan's gun hand tensed, and he began scanning the crowd in earnest. He thought he caught a glimpse of a Janx, but a small forest of people dressed as eight foot tall trees passed in between, and he couldn't be sure. His eyes darted back and forth across the hall, and soon he thought he caught another glimpse, but from the opposite side of the corridor. *How could Janx have moved that far in such a short time?* Perhaps Breegan was just seeing things. The crowd was a little thinner in the side hall, moving more quickly, but still, there were a large number of people, so many places for Janx to blend in and lose himself. Breegan could feel his heart pounding, both from the exertion of the run and from the anticipation of catching up to Janx. He tried to force himself to calm down.

"We're right on top of him," said Sam, almost whispering in her excitement. "We should be able to see him."

Both Sam and Breegan tensed, straining their senses to get a view of Janx, but both failing. Sam glanced down at her badge to check the map.

"Look out!" she said, "he's coming this way!" They stopped, bracing themselves for the attack, but none came. There was no Janx.

"He just passed us," she said, astonishment in her voice.

"What?" said Breegan. "Where?" He stood on

his toes, craning his neck to get a glimpse of Janx. "How could we miss him?"

"This way," said Sam, gesturing with her badge, her gun in her other hand. She followed the tiny red dot on the badge's map into a small convenience store that opened onto the hall. She pointed to a young man wearing a hooded sweatshirt who was picking through a candy rack. Sam and Breegan spread out to approach him from either side.

"Atlanta PD," Breegan said, showing his badge to the man. "I need to ask you some questions." The man froze, hands hovering over the chocolate bars, his body motionless. Only his eyes moved, shifting from Breegan's badge to his gun, and then to his face. The kid swallowed hard and blinked.

"I'm just trying to buy a candy bar, man," he said, but he remained motionless.

"That's all good and well," said Breegan," but where were you on the night of…" he searched his brain for a date…"January 12th of this year?"

"What?" said the man. "January 12th?"

The man stood still, his eyes looking up as he concentrated hard, trying to remember what he was doing on a random night several months ago. Breegan wondered, as he had many times in the past, why people look up when they're trying to remember something. As the man thought, Sam waved her badge in the general area that the man occupied, her circles growing smaller until she was focused on his head and then the back of his head. She holstered her gun and then reached out toward the man. He didn't move other than to close his eyes.

"That's an interesting cologne," said Sam, as she leaned in toward the young man. "Is that cilantro? Rosemary?" His eyes, clouded with confusion, snapped to her face, but he said nothing.

She reached into the hood on his sweatshirt and pulled out a small piece of electronic gadgetry. As she held it up for Breegan to see, realization dawned on both their faces. Breegan let out a long, low whistle and lowered his gun. After a moment, he dug his hand into an inner coat pocket and drew out a crumpled photo of Janx and showed it to the kid.

"Have you seen this...guy?" Breegan asked.

"Are you serious?" asked the kid. "There's a monster around every corner here!"

"Yeah, there are a lot of them, aren't there?" Breegan said, stuffing the picture back into his pocket. "It seems I don't have any other questions." The man peered at Breegan and then Sam. As Sam and Breegan focused their attention on the electronic piece, the man moved stealthily away from them, back out into the hallway, where he quickly vanished from sight, apparently having decided that he didn't need a candy bar after all.

"I told you Janx was hyper-intelligent," said Sam. "He's opened the device and removed the tracking element. He must've dropped it into that young man's hoodie, leading us on a…what do you say here? A wild turkey chase?" she said, grinning from ear to ear.

"Goose," said Breegan. "A wild goose chase." He holstered his gun and shoved his badge back into a coat pocket. "What are you grinning about?" he said, annoyed. "We can't track him now."

"That's true," she said, her grin turning into a broad, beaming smile. "But without this piece, he can't create a portal just anywhere." She looked at him expectantly, waiting for realization to dawn over him. She waited in vain.

"Without this piece in his possession, we don't need to track him; we know where he's going to be!" She slapped him on the shoulder and said, "He's trapped."

Chapter Twenty

SAM AND BREEGAN WERE sitting in a booth in a restaurant off the main lobby of the hotel. The sun had gone down, and the lobby took on an entirely different look now that the sunlight wasn't streaming in through the huge bank of skylights high above or through the wall of glass at the hotel entrance. Now the precisely designed lighting of the lobby cast pools of light to play with the shadows, creating a dramatic, moody feel to the opulent interior. The waiter put two cups of coffee on the table, one in front of each of them, and then dug into his apron. He pulled out a handful of tiny creamer cups and piled them unceremoniously on the table.

"Will there be anything else," he asked hope-fully, gloomily envisioning the tiny tip that would come, if any came at all, from an order of two cups of coffee.

"No, thanks," said Breegan, "We're good." The waiter gave a slightly sour smile and started to leave, muttering under his breath.

"Wait," said Breegan. "How late is the restaurant open?"

The waiter turned back toward the table and said, "Till eleven, sir." He hovered, hoping for a more substantial order and, therefore, a more substantial tip. After a moment, the waiter realized that no order was forthcoming, so he continued on his way back to the kitchen.

Breegan checked his watch as he picked up his coffee and started drinking, savoring the hot, bitter liquid.

"We may just have time for another cup before they close," he said.

Sam fiddled with the cups of creamer and the glass container of sugar that was on the table, huddled neatly together with the ketchup and a bottle of hot sauce that promised to cleanse one's colon.

"So just how, exactly, is he trapped?" Breegan asked.

"Well," she said, "Not caught completely. Not

totally unable to get away, not totally thwarted in his plans, if that's what you're hoping." As she spoke, she took experimental sips of the coffee, then added more creamer or sugar, trying to find the best combination. "We actually just got very lucky, Breegan. As you know, our badges let us teleport from anywhere, at any time. With your badge, Janx could've opened a portal at will, and we would've been pretty much scuppered..nothing we could do to stop him." She was starting to talk faster, the caffeine and sugar taking a grip on her physiology. She was rapidly draining her cup now and trying to flag down the waiter to bring another.

"Could we focus a little?" Breegan asked. He still marveled at the effect coffee had on her and wondered just how jaded his palate had to be to feel so little stimulation from his cup.

"Yes, right. Well, by pulling out the geo-locating device in the badge, the part that let us track him, he also pulled out the part that lets the badge teleport from any location. He has to rely on the astrophysical teleporting nodes now." She looked at him with satisfaction in her eyes. Breegan looked at her with an unimpressed one.

"Is there an English translation for that?" he

asked. "I mean, an English translation that I'm going to understand." He leaned toward the aisle of the restaurant and deftly flagged down the waiter, holding up his cup and pointing toward it. The waiter frowned and headed to the kitchen to grab the coffee pot.

"Yes, Breegan, I've told you this before. The alignment of celestial bodies…planets, stars, even comets…can cause nodes in space-time, areas where the conditions are optimal for creating a portal. Without the locating device from the badge, Janx can only open a portal at one of these nodes. And fortunately for us, we can calculate where such a node will be. We can and we have." She beamed at him and pulled a sheaf of paper from her coat, paper covered with her scribbled notes. She spread them on the table and paused in her explanation to re-concoct her creamer to sugar ratio in the cup the waiter had just refilled with steaming coffee.

"So we can figure out where Janx will be when he opens this portal?" Breegan asked. "How much good will that do us?"

"You really don't pay much attention, do you?" she said, somewhat annoyed. "Time and space are deeply connected. The calculations I conducted for the location of the portal also show the optimal time for the opening. It's not an exact science, mind you, but we do have a good idea of the time window. Plus or minus ten minutes or so."

"Look," she said, getting up and moving to his side of the booth, rearranging the pieces of paper so they both could see them from that side of the table. Breegan looked, but, knowing nothing about space-time mechanics or three-dimensional geometry, he couldn't make out anything from the seemingly endless scribbles of figures and diagrams.

"So the computer did most of the calculations, but then the results have to be fed into a space-time matrix. The computers at the library didn't have the proper software for that, and I didn't have a copy on me, so I had to do that part manually. That's what all this is," she said, using a finger to draw a circle around one area of the pages.

"I see," said Breegan, though he really didn't. He was still stinging from the annoyed tone in Sam's voice earlier and didn't want to appear too ignorant. He noticed that under the tables she indicated was a group of figures that had been circled several times.

"What is this?" he asked, pointing to them. "Is

this the location?" It was a guess, but it seemed reasonable enough.

"Yes!" she said, smiling at him. "Splendid! That is the location in four-dimensional terms. She looked at him with some pride in her eyes, like a tutor whose pupil is finally beginning to grasp the lesson.

"Four-dimensional?" he said.

"Yes, four. Three dimensions of space combined with the fourth dimension of time. Have you ever taken a science class?" she teased. He frowned slightly. His learning curve was steep.

"What does that translate into in….I dunno, Earth terms?" he asked.

"Basically it says midnight tonight, somewhere in this building, about 300 feet above street level. Hold on," she said, pulling out her badge. She opened it with the rhythmically tapped code and then began manipulating the central disk. She entered the coordinates from her pieces of paper and laid the badge on the table. On the disk, Breegan could see red digits and symbols dancing, swirling, combining, and separating. The badge chirped and a 3D holographic image of the hotel in which they were sitting appeared above the disk. The image showed the ground floor, a blinking red dot sitting in the booth that they occupied. As they watched, floors began appearing on top of each preceding floor, moving swiftly up through the building, the blinking dot leading the way. It quickly reached the top floor of the building, glowing red letters indicating the penthouse level. The red dot was centered in an area that, according to more red letters, was the Grand Ballroom.

"So," said Breegan, "midnight in the Grand Ballroom." He managed to make this sound like a confident statement and not a question. "That doesn't give us much time."

"No, we'll have to hurry, but it should be easy, right?" She said, grinning.

"Yes, because all of this has been easy, hasn't it?" He shook his head gently. The day's events had him confounded. Janx should never have been able to escape the transdimensional prison in the first place and then to wind up in this exact place, at this exact time, where a comic book convention would allow him to blend in seamlessly with his surroundings. In a world laden with technology so he could construct his own portal device. The odds definitely seemed stacked in Janx's favor.

"If I had to bet on things," he said, glumly, "I would have to consider just how good Janx's luck has been before I placed my bet. He's gotten the best of us at every turn."

"He *has* had a good run, hasn't he?" said Sam. "But his luck is turning. With these calculations, we finally have an advantage over him. Until now, we've been shooting in the dark. So let's not get all maudlin. Let's get to work."

She reached out and patted him on the shoulder encouragingly. Breegan looked up at her and smiled, not his best and brightest smile, but at least it was a smile.

"You're right," he said. "So we know where and when Janx will try to open his portal. Then what? How do we stop him?" He was still thinking about how Janx had defeated them every time they had an encounter.

"You leave that to me," she said, "I have an idea." She tapped and twirled her fingers on the disk of her badge. "I've sent the coordinates to your badge so you can see the precise location where he'll have to set up his portal."

"Right," said Breegan. "What are we going to do?"

"Come with me to the maintenance office. We need to create a little device of our own, but we'll need some tools. As you say, we don't have much time. Hurry up," she said, already on her feet and moving toward the door. Breegan hastily gulped down the last bit of his coffee and slapped a solitary dollar down on the table before he, too, jumped to his feet and hurried after her.

Chapter Twenty-One

"SO WHAT'S THIS ABOUT?" asked Breegan once they reached the privacy of the maintenance office. They both stood, Breegan leaning against one of the desks while Sam paced rapidly back and forth, the caffeine obviously still gripping her. The hotel staff had been instructed to stay out of the room while the detectives were working on the case, so Breegan and Sam had little worry of their conversation being overheard.

"I've got a plan," Sam said, beaming.

"So you keep saying. What is it?"

"It came to me while I was working out the maths for the portal location when I couldn't remember if you invert the one or you carry it over to the next column. I really should have paid more attention in Transdimensional Algebra Class!"

"I thought you said we were in a hurry." Breegan said with a frown. He wondered about the wisdom of letting Sam drink coffee.

"Right, start looking around for some tools while I explain. I need you to take that microwave apart." Breegan's first response was surprise, but then he wondered why this request, of all the things that had happened that day, should be surprising. So, after a brief mental struggle, he wasn't surprised at all and merely started rummaging through drawers, looking for a screwdriver.

"Anyway," Sam continued as she too began searching through drawers and cabinets, "the long and short of it is, I was trying to remember to whether to invert the one or carry it. Then I realized that we could invert the power beam connected to Janx's portal key and, thusly, change the directionality of his portal." As she spoke, she noticed a side room to the office that appeared to be a spare parts room. She disappeared into that room and Breegan could hear her noisily searching.

"What do you mean, exactly, by change the directionality?" he asked. He had found a screwdriver and was busily working his way into the innards of the microwave.

"You did unplug that thing before you started

poking it with a pointy metal object, didn't you?" she asked from the storage room.

"Of course," he said, surreptitiously unplugging the machine and looking to see if she could see him. "Do you think I'm an idiot?" He turned back to his work.

"Make sure you don't damage the magnetron. That's the part I need."

"What the hell is a magnetron?" he asked.

"Really?" she asked, somewhat annoyed. "Did you never take any particle physics?"

Breegan bristled but was speechless. He wasn't sure he even knew what particle physics was, and he was very positive he never took a class in it.

"It should be behind the keypad," she continued. "It's a box with a coil and a stubby tube sticking out one side. Disconnect the two wires, but be careful not to damage the coil."

"Certainly not," he said, mocking her British accent and suddenly he wondered why she had one.

There was a loud crash from the parts room, like a metallic avalanche.

"Ah ha!" she said. Breegan heard Sam shove a few things around before she reappeared, looking triumphant, her arms laden with a large box of wire and a short piece of heavy, black pipe.

"Thank the Seven Portals these maintenance types never dispose of anything!" She emptied her arms onto a table and brushed the dust from her sleeves. She sat down and picked up the piece of pipe. It was only a few inches long, apparently a piece of scrap from some repair, and Breegan wondered why anyone would bother to keep it around. More likely that just hadn't bothered to throw it out.

Sam took out her plasma gun and fiddled with a knob on one side of it, which Breegan hadn't noticed before. In one hand, she held the piece of pipe, and she carefully aimed the gun at it. When she pulled the trigger, a short, glowing beam emitted from the barrel. As she brought the beam into contact with the pipe, it sliced through the metal, leaving the edges glowing cherry red. A plume of acrid smoke wound its way toward the ceiling as she made another cut. When that cut was complete, a small section of the pipe fell to the floor with a clang, and she held up the remaining piece, proudly showing off her work. What was left of the pipe now resembled the letter "C" with a very narrow opening.

"The directionality?" he reminded her.

Sam sat down at a table and pulled the box of

wire near her. She started to wind the wire around the piece of pipe, leaving a tail of wire hanging loosely from the tight coils she was creating.

"Yes, well, portals have a direction. If you remember, whenever we've gone through a portal, we did just that. We went through from this side to that."

Her speech was interrupted periodically so she could grunt from the effort to make the coils as tight as she could.

"Portals are sort of like a one-way street. Depending upon how you set the device, the objects that go through can only go one direction. If we wanted to bring something from that side to this, we could, but we couldn't go the other direction at the same time. Does that make sense?" she asked.

"As much sense as any of this," he said, with a wry smile. He had the microwave in pieces now. He saw the magnetron, he guessed, but was a little nervous about damaging it. He proceeded cautiously.

"To be honest, I'm not completely sure of the science behind it, but the directionality is controlled by the polarity of the power being applied. Janx will have his portal set to bring objects from the other side. If we can reverse the polarity of the power beam, we can change it to send things from this side to that."

"Ha!" said Breegan. "We can use his own device to send him back to prison! I get it now." His eyes met Sam's and they shared a smile. A light was finally appearing at the end of the tunnel that began in the hotel basement that morning.

"Hand me that," said Sam, reaching out her hand for the magnetron he had finally extracted. Breegan put the magnetron in her hand, and she fit it into the gap in the pipe. She connected the two ends of the wire wrapping the pipe to the two lugs on the bottom of the magnetron. Then she grabbed a roll of silver duct tape and used it to secure the magnetron in place.

"There," she said. "That should just about do that." She held up the finished assembly for Breegan to admire. Not knowing what he was looking at, his admiration was not quite what she expected, though he made a few vaguely positive sounds and nodded appreciatively.

"What is it?" he asked.

"We, my friend, have just built a Transdimensional Direction Inverter. A "TDI" for short." She smiled proudly. Breegan smiled, too, but rather more confusedly.

"So what do we do with it?" he asked, realizing that, once again, he was showing his ignorance. It had been a humbling day for him, and he could tell that the day wasn't done with him yet.

"We have to get this into the power beam that will generate when he activates his portal," she said.

"Sounds simple enough."

"Yes, it does, doesn't it?" They gave each other knowing looks. This day had had a way of taking simple tasks and making them very complicated.

"It will be dangerous," she said, as if that concept was new to the day's events. "Not only do we have to dodge Janx to place the TDI, but once it's in place and the portal reverses, we have to be careful not to go through the portal ourselves."

Breegan pictured being transported into the Joob cell at the Transdimensional Prison, surrounded by Janx's tribe of hungry Joob. He didn't enjoy the picture.

"Yes," he said. "I can see where that would be a problem." He shook his head to dispel the images that had flooded into his mind.

"Listen," Breegan continued, "I'm sorry I lost my badge."

"Yes, well that was hardly your fault," said Sam. "Let me see your mobile." She held out her hand toward Breegan while digging in her pocket for the tracking piece that Janx had used to mislead them while he made his escape. Breegan dutifully pulled out his phone and handed it to her. Sam put his phone down on the desk and dug into an inner pocket, removing what looked like a small pocket knife. She unfolded a blade from one end and one from the other. Breegan could see that they weren't knife blades, more like some kind of screwdriver blades, but curiously shaped. She picked up Breegan's phone, and before he had time to protest, she attacked it with the tool. Sam was amazingly swift. Breegan's phone seemed to simply fall to pieces in her hands.

"What are you doing?" Breegan yelled.

"Calm down," said Sam. "I'm just making some modifications. We can't go back through the portal for the sole purpose of getting another badge for you, but by patching this module into your mobile, I can give you some of the functionality." She closed a blade on her pocket tool and pulled out another, which looked like a thin screwdriver with a wire protruding from the tip. Sam held up the module that Janx had ripped from Breegan's badge and examined the wires that dangled from it. One by one, she began hold the end of a wire to a point within the guts of Breegan's phone. When she was satisfied with the wire's placement, she touched the connection between the wire and the cell phone circuit board with the thin tip of the blade she had just opened on her pocket tool. As she did, the tip of the blade glowed, soldering the wire from the badge module to the selected point on the phone. Sam worked methodically and soon all the wires were attached.

"See if you can find some tape," she said. Breegan looked through drawers while Sam began to reassemble the phone. The module wouldn't fit inside the phone, so Sam led the wires out one side of the case, closing the case as much as she could.

"Here," said Breegan, handing Sam a roll of black duct tape. Sam took the tape and used it to secure the two halves of the phone together. She took one more piece of tape and secured the badge module to the back of the phone.

"Now for a little programming," muttered Sam as she typed furiously on the phone's screen.

"There! Not my best bit of work, I must say," said said, turning the phone over in her hand to examine it, "but it will do for now." She handed the phone back to Breegan who also took a moment to examine her handiwork.

"Is this going to void my warranty?" he asked, knowing the answer. He looked at his wristwatch and started.

"C'mon! We have to go," he said, heading toward the door. Sam stuffed the TDI into a coat pocket and followed.

Chapter Twenty-Two

_____

BY 11:30, SAM and Breegan were in the Grand Ballroom, high atop the hotel. The trip was convoluted. They could only ride the elevators so far up into the building. The final few floors required a slow, winding route up a series of escalators. Ride up a floor, walk to the next escalator, ride up to another floor. All this amongst a throng of costumed revelers, many already in a state of inebriation. Most were dressed in steampunk attire. It was the Steampunk Ball, after all. Women were mostly dressed in large hoop skirts, voluminous and flowing, with mandatory bustiers or corsets, and tiny fascinators perched at jaunty angles on their heads. The men dressed in formal Victorian suits, tails, ties, and top hats. Breegan had never seen so many handlebar mustaches in one place before. In addition to the steampunk costumes, there were people in regular 'con attire, superheroes, movie characters, and even one bright red steampunk devil, complete with pitchfork, pointy tail, and top hat. Neither Janx nor the two detectives would stand out too much in this crowd.

Once on the top floor, they crossed the foyer toward the ballroom. On one side, the area was closed off for a renovation project. Various crates and toolboxes were scattered around, and the walls were partly demolished, with large loops of bundled wire hung from openings in the ceiling tiles above. They moved past this area to the ballroom doors, where the doorman asked to see their convention passes. They showed their badges instead, and the man reluctantly allowed them to enter.

The central feature in the ballroom was a raised stage, where a steampunk band was churning out a thunderous tune. The band wore costumes that seemed to be a combination of steampunk and BDSM styles. Corsets with thigh high, gleaming leather boots, lace face masks in place of fascinators. One of the women was wearing not much at all except for strategically placed electrical tape and the lone male in the band was clad in tan Victorian jodhpurs, his bare chest adorned with a vest composed of leather straps connected by chrome rings. The band members manipulated various electronic instruments while behind them, on large screens, various images flashed, seemingly at random. A woman in Victorian dress, a parasol over her shoulder, followed by an abandoned steam locomotive, rusted and decaying, followed by a dead rabbit oozing fluid and writhing with maggots. The images seemed to have nothing to do with the current song, though Breegan had difficulty understanding the words. Two large Van de Graaff generators flanked the stage, snarling and spitting lightning to adjacent copper rods. Towering stacks of speakers added to the visual weight of the edifice. An unseen fog generator kept a steady blanket of white smoke drifting across the stage, tumbling over the edge of the platform, and out into the crowd of dancers.

There were many people on the dance floor, heads moving mostly in unison with the thumping music. Breegan took Sam by the elbow and led her through the crowd to a place off to one side of the stage. They were out of the general swirling mass on the dance floor, and the spot offered a good view of the room. From this vantage point, they could see that the stage was a temporary construction;

there was no backstage area, no way for Janx to enter the room from that direction. He would have to come through the front doors, just as Sam and Breegan had done.

"We should be able to see him from here," said Breegan. He pulled out his cobbled together cell phone and deftly opened it.

"You should see a new app on your home screen," said Sam. "It's named "TDPD Tools."

Breegan peered at his phone and found the app. He pressed the icon and found himself looking at a menu that was similar to the one he had become familiar with on his TDPD badge. He pressed an item on the menu, calling up the map that showed Sam's coordinates for the portal event. "According to this, he has to be on the stage to open the portal."

"Good," said Sam, looking around. "His portal key will need a power source to function. We need to find that."

"Already done," said Breegan. "You can see the band is getting all their power from this electrical panel." He gestured to a large, gray metal box recessed into the wall near where they stood. A jumble of thick electrical cords snaked their way from the box to the stage.

"Yes," said Sam, "I believe you're correct." She flashed him a grim smile of determination. "This is where I need to be when he tries to open his portal. Why don't you move to the other side of the stage, so we have a better view?" Breegan nodded and threaded his way through the dancers to an empty space near the stack of speakers on the other side of the stage. He leaned against the wall, crossed his arms, and scanned the crowd intently.

The dance floor surged and swirled with the music. Around the edges, tired revelers sat at tables, some talking animatedly, some slumping in their chairs, visibly worn out by the day's adventures. There was a steady movement of people in and out of the ballroom. Several times Breegan thought he saw Janx coming through the door, but each time it turned out to be just another costumed person. Most of the women had their hair piled high, with tiny fascinators on top, clinging at jaunty angles, and most of the men wore stovepipe hats, making almost everyone at least six feet tall.

As he inspected the gathering for Janx, Breegan was sometimes startled, sometimes impressed with the costumes that paraded before him. He was dazzled by one passing pair of people, covered in tiny blinking lights. One young lady walked by in a

Victorian gown that looked entirely normal until she was passing Breegan and he saw on her back a large box, which looked like a gigantic lantern with a pair of live birds inside. His gaze followed her as she continued across the room. When his eyes returned to the direction of the door, Breegan was startled to see Steampunk Jesus standing directly in front of him, a neon halo around his head, vacuum tubes glowing on his chest, and his right hand raised in benediction. Breegan simply stared while Jesus completed his blessing and moved into the crowd.

After a few minutes of watching, he was startled by a chirping sound in his ear. He had forgotten the translation device Sam had given him to wear. He looked across the stage at Sam. She was waving an arm to get his attention, holding up her open badge for him to see. When she saw Breegan was looking at her, she pointed at the badge and mouthed something to him. He pulled out his jury-rigged phone and saw that an indicator light was blinking. He opened the phone, and the chirping in his ear was replaced with Sam's voice. A window popped up in the TDPD app and he could see video of her face.

"He's certainly cutting it close, isn't he?" she asked. "It's five till midnight. He should be here by now."

"I don't see him anywhere," said Breegan, still scanning the crowd. "How long will it take him to set up his device?"

"Not long at all, but I wouldn't think he would just stroll in at the last second!" There was worry in her voice, a worry that Breegan shared.

"Well, keep watching," he said. They went back to watching but kept their vidphones on. Again, Breegan was teased by the glimpse of someone big and dark, but again it turned out not to be Janx. He began to pace back and forth within the small space he had to himself, scanning the crowd, checking his watch, scanning the crowd again. Still nothing. Two minutes till midnight. Breegan began to sweat that prickly, nervous sweat of anxiety.

"Bugger," he heard through his vidphone. "Damn and blast!"

"What is it?" Breegan asked. He started shoving his way through the crowd toward Sam, making no effort to be polite.

"I've made an error," she said, not seeming to want to give too much detail.

"Well, what is it? We don't have much time here."

"I made an error with my calculations. Four-dimensional maths never were my cup of tea," she was saying as he finally reached her side. He snapped his phone shut and thrust it into his pocket.

"Get to the point."

"Well, I've been rechecking my maths…I didn't think we both really needed to watch for an ominous character that would stand head and shoulders above most of the people here."

"The point!" He grabbed her by the shoulder and gave her a sharp shake. "It's midnight now!"

"I carried a sign incorrectly. The location is wrong. This isn't it!" Breegan let go of her shoulder and scraped his hand slowly across his five o'clock shadow, a sinking feeling growing his stomach.

"Do you know the correct one?" he asked, slowly.

"One more second. Let me feed these coordinates into the map." Sam furiously tapped entries into the central disk of her badge. Again the tiny red dot showed their current location and then, in a rapid blur, their view swooped down to the lowest floor of the building, where it blink placidly, indicating the correct location of the portal.

"That looks familiar," she said. They both peered at the map for a few seconds.

"That's the site of the original portal," said Breegan.

"That actually makes sense, come to think of it," said Sam in her usual, cheery voice. Breegan glared at her.

"So that's it?" he said. "We're through? We missed him?" He pictured an angry, hungry swarm of Joob streaming through the streets of Atlanta, slaughtering at will.

"Not necessarily," she said. "The time window lasts maybe twenty minutes, say ten before midnight to ten after. But I guess you're right…there's no way we can get there in just a couple of minutes." She looked dejected.

"I have an idea," he said. He grabbed her by the arm and began running out of the ballroom as quickly as the crowd would allow.

Chapter Twenty-Three

B REEGAN RUSHED ACROSS THE dance floor, Sam in tow. He yelled and waved his arms, shoving people out of the way with no thought of being nice. They were moving too quickly to listen to anyone's complaint, anyway. In just moments, they were exiting the ballroom, but instead of heading toward the escalators for the winding, zigzagging route down to the elevators, Breegan veered toward the construction site, tearing the "do not cross" tape with his free hand.

"Where are we going?" asked Sam, shrugging out of his grip now that they were free from the masses on the dance floor.

"This way," he said, without elaboration. He hurried through the construction area toward the windows. He came to a stop near a section of window where the glass had been removed and replaced with plywood sheets, a circular cutout in the middle.

"This is our elevator," he said, gesturing toward the hole, slightly out of breath.

"What do you mean?" she asked. "What is that?" She peered dubiously at the hole.

"It's a garbage chute," he said. "They use this to get construction debris down to the street level below. It will be a straight shot." He, too, was eying the hole somewhat suspiciously.

"Is it safe?" she asked, peering at him, trying to detect the truth.

"I have no idea," he said. "I've never tried this before, but it's our only chance of reaching the basement in time."

The looked at each other for a moment, wondering if this was actually happening. Which one would take the plunge first? Seconds ticked by.

"Come on," he said. "We don't have time to debate." He paused, swallowing as he regarded the yellow hole one more time. "I think the best policy is to keep your feet together and use your hands to press against the sides to slow yourself."

"You *think?*" she asked, incredulously. "You only *think?*" She glared at him, not knowing whether to take him seriously or not. Before she could make up her mind, he had jumped into the hole, shouting something unintelligible as he vanished from sight. She stared after him, watching the yellow chute undulate violently as Breegan's sounds quickly faded from hearing.

"Bloody Hell," she said and jumped after him. She yelled, too, out of bravado she would later tell people, though, at the time, there was a distinct note of terror in her voice. The yellow walls flashed by, a painful, rhythmic bumping ever present on her backside as she spiraled down through the never-ending chute, which was reinforced by some sort of hard cabling. She struggled to keep her feet together. She quickly pulled the sleeves of trench coat down over her hands so she could brace herself against the walls, just as Breegan had suggested.

A roaring wind rose to meet her as she plummeted; how fast she couldn't judge. The tails of her trench coat flapped around her head, making it hard to see. The chute was dusty, and Breegan's recent passage had stirred it up, forcing Sam to breathe in clouds of chalky powder. She gritted her teeth and focused on breathing through her nose.

Around and around she spun, growing a little

nauseated. Her backside screamed in pain as the constant thumping took its toll. She wondered just how much longer this punishment could go on, but there seemed to be no end. Lights flashed by on the outside of the chute, she assumed from the floors she was passing on her way down. The flashing was rapid, almost seizure-inducing, almost hypnotic, and she entered a state of mind where the fall seemed endless. She could scarcely remember a time when she wasn't falling, and she began to feel as though it were her lot in life to fall endlessly through a flashing, dusty, yellow tunnel. At one point it even felt as though she were falling upward.

Time expanded into an endless, Möbius strip of taffy, stretching and stretching, never breaking, never moving forward or backward, but endlessly moving. She thought she would pass out or vomit or both. She closed her eyes and concentrated on keeping her throat shut, to keep the bile down. She could barely stand the fine, powdery, dusty taste of drywall talc in her throat, even though she was breathing through her nose. Sam felt herself beginning to black out, the edges of her consciousness closing in, a final, fatal constricting vignette to her life. She wasn't going to make it.

Suddenly, she rolled out into a dumpster on the

street level. She somersaulted several times in an even more disorienting manner, coming to a rest flat on her back in a cloud of dust. Fortunately, the last things that had been sent down the garbage chute before them were carpet scraps and carpet padding, a reasonably soft, if smelly, landing mat for their decent. Sam groaned and lifted her head, looking around. Breegan stood to one side of the dumpster, leaning against the metal wall, rubbing his backside with one hand.

"Well," she said, chuckling. "That was interesting."

"Shut up and come on," said Breegan. He struggled to wade through the debris toward a low wall at the back of the dumpster. "We still have to get to the basement."

"Remind me not to have you schedule my holiday for me," she groaned, pulling herself upright and lurching after him. They reached the lower wall of the dumpster and climbed over. They moved as quickly as their thrashed bodies could manage. Their maneuvers weren't entirely impressive. It was like watching a couple of zombies race each other down an alley. But they moved more quickly as their joints loosened up after the traumatic decent from thirty flights up. They reached a pair of doors that gave access to the basement, but there were no handles on the outside.

"Ugh. The doors can't be opened from the outside," said Sam. She stood, hands on hips, breathing deeply. They looked up and down the building, searching for a way to get inside.

"Here we are," said Breegan, pointing to a ground level window on the side of the building. He put a hand on the wall to steady himself and swung a mighty kick at the window. It gave way with a tinkling of shattered glass. Breegan shook his leg to make sure there was no glass left on him and then took off his coat. He quickly wrapped it around his hand and broke out the rest of the glass that was still attached to the frame. He shook out his coat and pulled it back on. Then he gestured cavalierly with one hand.

"After you," he said. Sam smiled a dubious smile, dropped down to the ground, and scrambled through the opening. Breegan quickly followed.

Chapter Twenty-Four

B REEGAN DROPPED DOWN THROUGH the empty window frame and landed with a soft crunch on the shattered glass on the concrete floor below. He landed in a squatting position, one hand on the ground, the other on the wall. He held that position for a moment trying to orient himself. Sam was already moving down the hall in front of him, coattails streaming out behind her. Breegan stood with more effort than he would like to admit and scrambled to catch up with her.

The hallway was crowded with a random collection of hotel detritus. Old, broken chairs, stacks of empty milk crates, a laundry cart full of dirty table cloths, and a collection of chrome poles and sagging velvet ropes standing in a jumble, like a pack of forlorn circus clowns after the big top is torn down. The hall was not as clean as Breegan might have supposed, having viewed the immaculate public side of the hotel above them, and an odor of spoiled milk pervaded the air.

"Look for a stairwell," he said, out of breath and sweating. He moved with a slight stagger, the vertiginous effects of their decent still reeling his brain. He had had no time to recover and thought briefly that he might want to reconsider drinking and smoking and generally not doing anything to get into, or remain in, shape. He reached out to steady himself against the wall and pushed on, still rushing to beat the clock.

"Here it is," said Sam, cutting across the hallway and slamming open the door. They plunged down the stairwell as quickly as they could, footsteps rasping out a rough staccato on the gritty stairs. Fortunately, the lighting was working fine, and they didn't have to deal with the confusing effects of jerking flashlights in the angular stairwell. The cooler air of the subterranean levels rushed up to greet them as they descended. Again they spun around the spiral of the stairs, thankfully less quickly than they did tumbling down the garbage chute. As they approached the final steps, Breegan snatched at Sam's sleeve, reining her in.

"Shh," he said, "we may still be able to surprise him." He made a gesture with his free hand, meant to convey meaning just in case the words didn't.

"Right. We still need to hurry. Watch the shadows," she said and eased open the door. They slipped through the doorway, trying to move as quickly and quietly as they could. The hall stretched out in front of them, the lights spaced out in this little-used portion of the building. The spacing caused the light in the hall to pool in spots, while the shadows pooled in others. At random intervals, hallways and doorways opened onto the main hall, and it was obvious that Janx had numerous hiding spaces. Breegan pulled out his gun. Sam caught the glint of light on the barrel.

"Put that away," she said, digging in her pocket. Sam pulled out her snub-nosed plasma gun and shoved it in his direction. "Use this instead. It will be much more effective." She shot him a grim smile as he accepted her weapon and returned his own to its holster. "Turn that knob to the little triangle symbol," she said. Breegan glanced down at the weapon and did as she told him.

Ahead of them, they could see the power distribution block and the hole in the masonry wall where the day's events began. Yellow police tape crisscrossed the area, though the police guard was no longer there. Sam got her badge out and tapped it open as they continued down the hall. She tapped some other code onto the black disk and then held the badge out in front of her, sweeping it back and forth gently, apparently scanning for something.

"What are you doing?" hissed Breegan. He kept his head swiveling, his eyes never resting on one spot for long.

"Looking for the energy signature of a portal being opened," she said. "I don't see anything yet. Nor do I see any residual energy from a recently closed portal. He's not here yet." They spread out across the hallway and began to look around more closely. Breegan kept his weapon trained where his eyes were, pivoting rapidly to check in all directions.

"I don't see anything," said Breegan, relaxing his stance a little. "We are sure about the math this time, aren't we?" he asked, not a little sarcastic. Sam stood near the power block. She glanced around one more time, looking disgusted, and then dug into her pockets for her scribbled notes. She started triple-checking her figures. Breegan moved over to peer at the sheets, too. He wasn't quite sure why, because he was quite certain he didn't know the first thing about the kind of mathematics she was using.

Just as he reached Sam's side, he caught a movement out of the corner of his eye, the flicker of shadow in motion.

Breegan whirled, snapping the gun up, prepared to fire, but Janx moved even faster. Janx let out a roar that thundered down the hall and swung an incredibly muscled arm at Breegan. Breegan fired just as Janx struck him. The shot went wild. A portion of the wall above Janx's head exploded in a shower of blue sparks, bits of rock, and masonry dust as Breegan flew across the hall and hit the wall with a dull thud. He crumpled to the floor in a motionless pile at the base of the power distribution block. Sam's gun skidded across the floor and came to rest against the wall on the other side of the hallway.

Sam looked up just as Janx sent Breegan sprawling. She instinctively felt for her gun, forgetting she had given it to Breegan. She managed to take a step back before the next swing came her way. Janx's arm was as solid as a baseball bat. Sam heard something crack and felt a sharp pain stabbing her in the side as all her breath was forced violently from her lungs. She was thrown against the opposite wall. Gravity tightened its grip and Sam fell to the ground and then she, too, lay still on the floor. Janx snorted and considered them both for a moment.

"So weak," he said. He reached into his shirt and pulled out his makeshift portal key, a lumpy, misshapen conglomeration of misfit parts. He walked toward the hole in the wall, ripping down the police tape as he went.

Chapter Twenty-Five

J ANX STRODE PURPOSEFULLY TOWARD the hole in the basement wall where, just a few hours earlier, he had first made an appearance into this world, this Earth. In the span of one Earth day, his fortunes had changed from dismal to most excellent, from a prisoner with a life sentence and no chance of parole, to a free Joob on the verge of setting free his entire tribe to rule over the puny species inhabiting this world. Janx was never one to question his manifest superiority over all things, and it was events just like today's that merely served to reinforce his confidence.

"Today I will avenge myself and my people!" he said to the crumpled forms lying on the floor. "And it will be so easy." He chuckled his deep, chest vibrating chuckle, his eyes gleaming with anticipation. Both Breegan and Sam lay silent and motionless. Janx walked to the place where he first entered this dimension, kicking aside some of the scattered bits of rubble lying on the floor. He faced the hole in the wall and began to press buttons on his cobbled together device. Though his hands and fingers were quite large, he seemed to have no trouble pushing the tiny buttons on the keypad Janx had apparently swiped from a basic cell phone. The device lit up and made quiet chirping noises in response to his touch. The device had two screens, attached at strange angles, and a short, stubby antenna poking out at an entirely different angle.

Behind him, Breegan cracked open his eyes and tried to focus them on the scene before him. He could only see blobs of shadow and blurry splashes of light. The glare hurt his eyes, and the realization of that fact made him conscious of his other pains. He ached over a good deal of his body, and he could taste blood in his mouth, but he didn't seem to be too badly hurt. Fortunately, he remembered clearly where he was, and so he lay as still as he could while he tried to locate Janx. His vision was returning slowly. He blinked a few times and squinted a little. He could see Sam's coat lying on the floor across the hallway from where he was.

Why is her coat on the floor? he thought. Just then the coat moved a tiny bit, and he realized that it was Sam lying there, not just her coat. She must've been hit, too. He squinted hard and blinked a few more times. His vision was almost completely clear now, and he could see Janx standing with his back to the hallway, apparently fiddling with something.

Sam, too, was beginning to stir. Like Brregan, she felt sore all over, but she could also feel a sharp pain in her side, a pain that increased dramatically whenever she took a breath. *Broken ribs,* she thought and tried to keep her breathing shallow and even. She felt another pain in her stomach and wondered if she might have ruptured an organ, but then realized she was lying on something, the Transdimensional Direction Inverter. She tried to shift her body to get the TDI out from under herself, but the effort brought a spasm of pain surging through her body, and she gasped aloud.

Janx instantly jerked his head in her direction, glaring at her but not even bothering to turn his body to face her. Satisfied that she neither Breegan nor Sam was on their feet, he turned back to his device, tapped in a few more keystrokes, and then turned to face Sam.

"So," he said, with his voice like an echo from the seventh circle of hell, "You're not quite dead yet, are you? It's just as well. My brethren will be hungry, and it's been such a very long time since they've had fresh non-synthetic blood. They will find you to be a pleasant change of diet." He turned his attention back to the portal device.

Sam shifted her weight again, this time taking a shallow breath, then holding it to brace herself for the pain. She managed to get the TDI out of from under her body but kept it concealed in her pocket. Her mind raced for a way to get the inverter into the power beam that would soon connect to Janx's key. She could barely shift her body, let alone jump up and dash across the hall to be between Janx's portal device and the power block. She looked for Breegan, wondering what had happened to him. She scanned the corridor and saw that he was lying at the base of the power block, unmoving, apparently lifeless.

The display on Janx's key began blinking a green light at him. He smiled, pressed one last button on the device, and placed it on the ground at his feet. He took a step back and put his hands on his hips.

"The time is now, detectives. You have failed." Smug satisfaction dripped from his voice. At his feet, the device chirped and then beeped a slow, measured cadence. It began to glow, faintly at first and then brighter. It began to hum, too, the sound growing with the brightness of the display. A tendril of lightning reached out from the device toward the power distribution block. A mirror image of the lightning reached out from the block toward the device. Suddenly the two tiny bolts of lightning connected. When they did, the light and the hum grew exponentially; the lightning bolts became as thick as a person's arm, snapping and crackling with energy. Above the device, floating in midair, appeared a black void, a blackness that emitted no light and seemed to absorb the light around it. At the edges, blue-white lightning danced. An icy wind began to blow from the center of the void, gently at first and then rapidly gaining in force and velocity.

"While we wait on this, I think I'll take care of you," said Janx, focusing on Sam and moving in her direction. Her mind raced, not knowing what to do. Her right hand was in the pocket of her coat, fingers wrapped around the inverter but no plan came to her, no scheme to place it.

The void had grown to almost fill the height of the hallway; the lightning fringe had become an impressive fireworks display. In the center, an image appeared. Sam could see a crowd of Joob, huddled together as if posing for a group photo, snarling and roaring, eager to feast. In mere moments the portal would be completely opened, unleashing the Joob upon the unsuspecting Earth.

Janx stopped in front of her and reached down, grabbing the lapels of her coat. He lifted her effort-lessly until her eyes were on the same level as his. Sam frantically looked around, powerless to escape his grasp, powerless to alter the coming events. She winced in pain from her broken ribs and cried out.

"Perhaps I'll just drain you myself," said Janx. "There are plenty of others for my brethren." He started to lift her high enough to skewer her on his horn. Sam cast one final glance at Breegan and was startled to see that he was looking at her, making a "come here" gesture with his hands. Sam jerked the inverter out of her pocket and tossed it across the hall to Breegan. Sam had thrown wide, and Breegan pushed his feet hard against the power block, sliding his body across the floor. He caught the inverter with one hand and snatched up Sam's gun with the other. He thrust the inverter up into the power beam that arced between the power block and Janx's key. Instantly the blue power beam turned red, as did the lightning dancing around the edges of the void. The wind too reversed itself and began sucking into the void instead of blowing out.

Breegan took rapid but careful aim with the weapon. He squeezed off a shot, the blue plasma beam lighting up the hall as it grazed Janx's arm and punched a large hole in the wall behind, showering sparks and debris down into the hallway. Janx howled with a combination of rage and pain and dropped Sam.

"Grab onto something!" Sam yelled. Breegan scrambled back toward the power block and wrapped an arm around one of the legs supporting it. He felt the vortex starting to pull him into the portal. Sam clutched at the door frame where she had fallen at Janx's feet. Janx spun to face Breegan, struggling to keep his footing in the growing hurricane of wind.

"What have you done?" he shouted, his voice nearly drowned by the howling wind. Sam tightened her grip on the door and lashed out at hard as she could, kicking at Janx's feet. She didn't have much strength, and the effort left her whimpering in pain, but it was enough to knock Janx off balance. He stumbled, and the wind took hold of him, sucking him toward the portal. Breegan and Sam, too, were being pulled toward the void, their arms straining to hold their positions, bodies stretched out across the floor.

"No!" Janx screamed. His hands flailed wildly, desperately trying to find something, anything, to grab onto as he slid across the floor toward the swirling vortex. But he found nothing. The wind pulled him off his feet, and he tumbled through the air into the center of the portal. As he passed through, the portal emitted a blinding flash of light, and the power went out.

Instantly, the wind started to abate. Breegan unhooked his arms from around the power block and lay panting on the floor. As the emergency lighting flickered on, he could see Sam lying on the floor across the hall, curled into a ball, her arms wrapped around her ribcage. Breegan slowly pushed himself into a seated position, feeling every ache and bruise from the day's events. He shifted until his back was against the wall and then he tipped his head back, closed his eyes, and waited for some strength to come back to his limbs.

Sam sat up slowly, keeping one arm wrapped around her ribs, steadying herself with the other. She, too, leaned back against the wall. They looked at each other, exchanging grim smiles, exhaustion and bruises preventing them from much celebration.

After several minutes, Breegan staggered to his feet. He turned to the circuit breakers on the power block. He pulled on the tripped lever and grunted as he reset the switch. The power block gave a satisfied clunk, and the main lights came back on. He walked over to Sam and held out a hand. She took it, and he gently pulled her to her feet.

"Are you ok?" he asked. He looked her over and decided that, although worse for wear, she didn't look critically injured.

"I think he broke some ribs, but other than that I'm the bees knees," she said, grimacing as the pain in her side reminded her not to speak. "Have you got a ciggy?" she asked.

Breegan patted down his coat pockets and found his pack of cigarettes. He performed his ritual smack and grab, pulling two cigarettes out and placing them in his mouth. He lit them both and then took one and put it gently between Sam's lips.

"Ta," she said. They both inhaled, though Sam did so gingerly, and released a bluish cloud into the air.

They turned to look at the hole in the wall where the portal had been, but the hole was gone. The debris that had been scattered around the floor was neatly back in place in the wall. Not even cracks remained where the cinder blocks had been broken, and the floor looked like it had been swept recently. Someone who hadn't seen the earlier destruction would never suspect the wall had been breached at all.

"Is it supposed to be like that?" said Breegan.

"Bugger me if I know," Sam said. "I never was much good at all that science stuff." She walked over to Janx's portal key, still lying on the floor, and gingerly bent to pick it up. She winced as she stood, turning the device over to examine it.

"Ingenious, really," Sam said and then pocketed the device. "This," she said, gesturing to the wall, "will actually make it very easy to deny everything." Breegan looked at her, wondering if she was serious. But then he smiled and ran a hand through his hair.

"I suppose denying it will be easier than trying to explain it."

Chapter Twenty-Six

STEVE WAS BURIED THE following Tuesday, a cold, rainy, and otherwise thoroughly miserable day. It was a simple graveside affair, with the excavated dirt draped in green outdoor carpet as if that could convince everyone of the normalcy of the event. There were no chairs or even a canopy, just the bereaved huddled together under dripping umbrellas. The trees were black and glistening, silent ghouls witnessing the proceedings. The rain fell in slow, fat, heavy drops, creating a dull staccato that played counterpart to the pastor's monotone drone. A chilling breeze gusted through the cemetery, sending occasional shivers down Breegan's back and causing him to think about how cold eternity would be, locked inside a steel box, six feet underground.

There were few people in attendance. Apart from Steve's widowed mother and two elderly ladies that accompanied her, there was no one else besides the pastor, the funeral home crew, and the honor guard from the police department, quietly and precisely folding the flag from Steve's coffin to present to his mother. Apparently, Steve had as many friends as Breegan did. Breegan and Sam stood a short distance away from the graveside, somberly watching the proceedings from the scant shelter provided by a clump of evergreen trees. Both knew that if not for a thin slice of luck, they, too, might be lying in their own caskets. Events hinge on the smallest of details. The path of life can take a new direction at any moment.

Although it was unofficially "cold," the case file was officially still open. There was not much work being done at this point. No solid evidence had been found of the killer, no arrest had been made. There was not even a suspect, though the killings had stopped as abruptly and mysteriously as they had started. Breegan, of course, knew that the case was closed but had not included all that he knew in his report. Although Steve technically had died in the line of duty, there was no prominent announcement in the papers, no tremendous outpouring of public dismay over his death, no ostentatious public funeral of a fallen hero. The department was keeping this as quiet as it could, which in this case was almost silent.

It was something of a black mark on Breegan's record, though, strangely, he didn't mind. Knowing what had happened and the disaster that they actually did prevent, he was satisfied with the results, even though he couldn't give a full explanation to his superiors. Not only could he not show them proof of transdimensional travel or a transdimensional demon, he felt sure that to even launch into an explanation of the events of the case would land him in the local psych ward for an extended vacation. The wisest course seemed to be to let the unsolved case go on his record. Truthfully, he felt more satisfied with this case, apart from Steve's death, than he had felt with a case in a long, long time.

Breegan's jaw clenched as an officer from the honor guard bent down to present the flag and then stood at attention to salute Steve's mother. She sobbed quietly, her two friends consoling her. Breegan was no soft touch, but he felt his eyes welling up and a tight feeling in his throat. Sam placed a hand on Breegan's back, and he turned to look at her. No words were needed, but he nodded at her in thanks as he blinked hard. The casket was lowered into the grave, and the mother moved closer to throw a handful of dirt down on top of it. Breegan watched her trembling hand hesitantly open to release the dirt, reluctant to let go of her only son.

The pastor said a final prayer and the funeral party moved away from the grave toward warm, dry vehicles, leaving the ghoulish trees to their vigil. Breegan and Sam walked through the squelching grass to stand near the grave. The crew from the funeral home had begun to remove the covering from the mound of dirt and disassemble the lowering device for the casket. They glanced curiously at the pair but continued in their work. Breegan fished a pack of cigarettes out of his coat pocket, once again performed his smack and grab routine, and offered one to Sam, which she accepted. She had her lighter ready and reciprocated by lighting his cigarette first, then hers. They took long drags, savoring the heat, and contemplating the recent events. The gusting wind dissipated their exhaled clouds quickly.

"Not sure we would've cracked this without his help," Breegan said.

"Yes," said Sam. "He did some excellent work."

"It's funny. We never met outside of work. I don't even know his mother's name. But he was my last friend on Earth. My wife's left; my parents passed away years ago and I have no brothers or sisters. Now this." Sam said nothing but put a hand on his shoulder.

"I never thought much about the people around me. Guess it's too late to worry about that now." Breegan bowed his head, gazing down into the grave at Steve's coffin, a coffin he never thought he would see, a coffin that he might be filling had events turned out slightly differently. He turned to look at Sam.

"Thanks," he said. He gave Sam a tight-lipped smile. "Thanks for saving my life back there."

"Ha!" she laughed. "Thank you! And thank Steve. Without the two of you, this probably would've turned out much differently. Much worse." She took her hand from his back, then slapped it, playfully. Breegan offered Sam his arm, which she took, and together they squelched their way toward his waiting car.

"Buck up," she said, her infectious smile returning. "We just saved your world! Now let's get out of the rain and find some hot coffee."

Epilogue

THEY WERE BACK IN cell block 7a, the permanent home of the Joob. Sam sat on a table, sipping a cup of coffee and gazing serenely through the window into the cell. Breegan stood nearby, also drinking coffee.

"This is pretty good," he said, raising his cup a little in case Sam didn't understand his meaning. "I thought you said you didn't have coffee here?"

"We didn't," she said, smiling slowly, "but we do now. Or at least *I* do. I haven't decided if I'm going to share this secret with anyone just yet." They laughed quietly.

"Success to crime," Breegan said, raising his cup in a toast. Sam raised hers, too, and they held each other's gaze for a moment, fully aware of the near disaster they had averted. They drank simultaneously, savoring the coffee, savoring their success. They turned to look out the windows again. Sam touched the glass, and a luminous control panel appeared. She tapped a few commands, and the window zoomed in on a clearing some ways off in the distance. There they could see Janx thrashing about, tearing down branches from the trees, throwing things, and generally displaying his displeasure. The other Joob shrunk from him as his continued his rampage. The zoomed in screen provided sound so they could hear his bellowing, as well. Sam made a quick motion on the glass, muting his bellowing.

"How are your ribs," Breegan asked.

"Fine," Sam said. "They've given me something for the pain and hit them with a subcutaneous fuser. They're mended now, but they'll be sore for a couple more days. I don't even get any time off!" She shrugged. It was all part of the job. Truthfully, she relished these moments of excitement bordering on terror. Otherwise, the job could be a bit dull and monotonous.

"Well, I guess I should be getting back," he said, though he made no real effort to move. He slowly reached into the inside breast pocket of his coat and drew out cobbled together cell phone.

He pointed to the tracking device Sam had grafted on and said, "I guess you'll be wanting this back."

"That reminds me," she said, "I wanted to talk to you about something." She turned to face him squarely, and his curiosity piqued.

"I was thinking we work well together. Once you overcame your initial doubts, I could see that you have some real skill as a detective." He chuckled. *Damn straight I do*, he thought. If she noticed his amusement, she made no sign of it.

"It occured to me," she continued, "that you might be a little bored with your work there, that it might have grown a little stale for you."

"Something like that had crossed my mind," he said, nodding. "To be honest, I've been thinking about throwing in the towel, retiring, maybe moving to Key West, taking up deep sea fishing."

"It also occurs to me that you found our little adventure a bit more…interesting…than your run-of-the-mill homicide. Is that correct?"

"Yes, now that you mention it. This case certainly had a few twists I hadn't seen before." He rubbed his chin. He could see where this was going, and he wasn't entirely opposed to the idea.

"Then why don't you stay?" she asked. "We

could work together. We make a great team!" She was enthused and couldn't hide the fact.

"Stay here?" he said, incredulous though he felt that this was what she had been leading up to all along. "How could I possibly do that?" he asked.

"You told me you have no family, no real friends. You just admitted that you were ready to retire there. What's there to stop you from coming here?" she asked.

He paused, his free hand still perched on his chin. She had a point. He had no real ties back there. And the work here certainly was more stimulating. He vacillated for a few more moments, feeling the rush of decision sweeping him along, barely in control. He grinned and thrust out his hand to shake hers.

"This looks like the beginning of a beautiful friendship."

About the Author

D.W. Dibling is an Adventure Librarian by day, Passionate Scribbler by night. In his mind, he lives by himself in the sprawl that is Atlanta, Georgia, contemplating a cat that preferably is hypoallergenic, knows how to use a toilet, and does not claw the numerous musical instruments scattered around his apartment. Whilst traveling the globe as a military guitar player, he managed to over-degree himself before he realized that his life-long dream of being a writer needed more serious attention.

www.diblingscribbling.com
dean@diblingscribbling.com